GREEK LESSONS

GREEK LESSONS

A Novel

—

HAN KANG

TRANSLATED BY
DEBORAH SMITH AND EMILY YAE WON

HOGARTH
LONDON / NEW YORK

Translation copyright © 2023 by Deborah Smith

Published in the United States by Hogarth, an imprint of Random House, a division of Penguin Random House LLC, New York.

HOGARTH is a trademark of the Random House Group Limited, and the H colophon is a trademark of Penguin Random House LLC.

Originally published in Korean as 희랍어 시간, or *Huilabeo Sigan* by Munhakdongne, Paju-si, South Korea, in 2011. Copyright © 2011 by Han Kang. This translation published in the United Kingdom by Hamish Hamilton, an imprint of Penguin Books, part of the Penguin Random House group of companies.

Hardback ISBN: 9780593595275
Ebook ISBN: 9780593595282

PRINTED IN CANADA ON ACID-FREE PAPER

randomhousebooks.com

2 4 6 8 9 7 5 3

GREEK LESSONS

1

As his dying wish, Borges requested the epitaph "He took the sword and laid the naked metal between them." He asked this of María Kodama, his beautiful, younger wife and literary secretary, who had married Borges two months before he died, at the age of eighty-seven. He chose Geneva as the place of his passing: it was the city where he had spent his youth and where he now wanted to be buried.

One researcher described that epitaph as "a blue-steel symbol." For him, the image of the blade was the key that would unlock the significance of Borges's writing—the knife that divides Borges's style from conventional literary realism—whereas for me, it seemed an extremely quiet and private confession.

The line was a quotation from a Norse saga. On the first night a man and a woman spent together (which, in this saga, was also to be their last), a sword was placed between them and left there until dawn. If that "blue-steel" blade was not the blindness that lay between the aging Borges and the world, then what was it?

Though I'd traveled to Switzerland, I didn't visit Geneva. I had no strong desire to see his grave firsthand. Instead, I looked around the library of Saint Gall, which he would have found endlessly enrapturing had he seen it (I recall the rough feeling of the felt slippers that visitors were given in order to protect the thousand-year-old library's floor), caught a boat at the wharf in Lucerne and floated through the valleys of ice-covered Alps until dusk.

I didn't take any photographs. The sights were recorded only in my eyes. The sounds, smells and tactile sensations that a camera cannot capture in any case were impressed on my ears, nose, face and hands. There was not yet a knife between me and the world, so at the time this was enough.

2

Silence

The woman brings her hands together in front of her chest. Frowns, and looks up at the blackboard.

"Okay, read it out," the man with the thick-lensed, silver-rimmed spectacles says with a smile.

The woman's lips twitch. She moistens her lower lip with the tip of her tongue. In front of her chest, her hands are quietly restless. She opens her mouth, and closes it again. She holds her breath, then exhales deeply. The man steps back toward the blackboard and patiently asks her again to read.

The woman's eyelids tremble. Like insects' wings rubbing briskly together. The woman closes her eyes, reopens them. As if she hopes in the moment of opening her eyes to find herself transported to some other location.

The man readjusts his glasses, his fingers thickly floured with white chalk.

"Come on now, out loud."

The woman wears a high-necked black sweater and black trousers. The jacket she's hung on her chair is black, and the scarf she's put in her big, black cloth bag is knitted from black wool. Above that somber uniform, which makes it seem as if she's just come from a funeral, her face is thin and drawn, like the elongated features of certain clay sculptures.

She is a woman neither young nor particularly beautiful. Her eyes have an intelligent look, but the constant spasming of her eyelids makes this hard to perceive. Her back and shoulders are permanently drawn in, as though she is seeking refuge inside her black clothes, and her fingernails are clipped back severely. Around her left wrist is a dark purple velvet hairband, the solitary point of color on an otherwise monochrome figure.

"Let's all read it together." The man cannot wait for the woman any longer. He moves his gaze over the baby-faced university student who sits in the same row as the woman, the middle-aged man half hidden behind a pillar and the well-set-up young man sitting by the window, slouching in his chair.

"Emos, hēmeteros. 'My,' 'our.'" The three students read, their voices low and shy. "Sos, humeteros. 'Your' singular, 'your' plural."

The man standing by the blackboard looks to be in his mid to late thirties. He is slight, with eyebrows like bold accents over his eyes and a deep groove at the base of his nose. A faint smile of restrained emotion plays around his mouth. His dark brown corduroy jacket has fawn-colored leather elbow patches. The sleeves are a bit short, exposing his wrists. The woman gazes up at the scar that runs in a slender pale curve from the edge of his left eyelid to the edge of his mouth. When she'd seen it in their first lesson, she'd thought of it as marking where tears had once flowed.

Behind thick, pale green lenses, the man's eyes are fixed on the woman's tightly shut mouth. The smile vanishes. His expression stiffens. He turns to the blackboard and dashes off a short sentence in Ancient Greek. Before he has time to add the diacritical marks, the chalk snaps and both halves fall to the floor.

.

Late spring of the previous year, the woman had herself been standing at a blackboard, one chalk-dusted hand pressed against it. When a minute or so had passed and she was still unable to produce the next word, her students had started to shift in their seats and mutter among themselves. Glaring fiercely, she saw neither students, nor ceiling, nor window, only the empty air in front of her.

"Are you okay, seonsaengnim?" asked the young woman with the curly hair and sweet eyes who sat at the very front of the class. The woman had tried to force a smile, but all that happened was that her eyelids spasmed for a while. Trembling lips pressed firmly together, she muttered to herself from somewhere deeper than her tongue and throat: *It's come back.*

The students, a little over forty in number, looked at each other with raised eyebrows. *What's she up to?* Whispered questions spread from desk to desk. The only thing she was able to do was to walk calmly out of the classroom. Exerting herself, she managed it. The moment she stepped out into the corridor, the hushed whispers became clamorous, as though amplified through a loudspeaker, swallowing the sound her shoes made against the stone floor.

———————

After graduating from university the woman had worked first for a book publisher and then at an editorial and production company for a little over six years; and after that she spent close to seven years lecturing in literature at a couple of universities and an arts secondary school in and around the capital. She produced three collections of serious poetry, which came out at three- or four-year intervals, and for several years had contributed a column to a fortnightly literary review. Recently, as one of the founding members of a culture magazine whose title had yet to be decided, she'd been attending editorial meetings every Wednesday afternoon.

Now that it had come back, she had no choice but to abandon all such things.

There had been no indication that it might happen, and there was no reason why it should have happened.

Of course, it was true that she'd lost her mother six months previously, divorced several years earlier still, had eventually lost custody of her eight-year-old son, and it was coming on five months since he had moved in with her ex-husband, after a prolonged battle in the courts. The grey-haired psychotherapist she'd seen once a week because of insomnia after the boy's departure couldn't understand why she denied such clear causes.

No, she wrote, using the blank paper left out on the table. *It isn't as simple as that.*

That was their final session. Psychotherapy conducted through writing took too long, with too much scope for misunderstanding. She politely turned down his proposal to introduce her to a speech and language therapist. More than anything else, she lacked the finances to continue with such expensive treatment.

·

As a young girl, the woman had apparently been "really bright"— something that her mother, during her final year of cancer treatment, had taken every opportunity to remind the woman of. As though, before she died, this was the one thing she had to make absolutely clear.

When it came to language, that label might have been true. By the age of four, and without being taught, she had a good grasp of Hangul. Knowing nothing of consonants and vowels, she'd memorized syllables as entire units. The year she turned six, her elder brother gave her an explanation of Hangul's structure, parroting what his teacher had said. As she listened, everything had seemed vague, yet she ended up spending that entire afternoon in early spring squatting in the yard, preoccupied by thoughts of consonants and vowels. That was when she discovered the subtle difference between the ㄴ sound as pronounced in the word 나, na, and when pronounced in 니, nih; after that, she realized ㅅ sounded different in 사, sah, than it did in 시, shi. Making a mental run-through of all the possible diphthong combinations, she found that the only one that didn't exist in her language was ㅣ, ih, combined with ㅡ, eu, and in that order, which was why there was no way of writing it.

Those trivial discoveries had been for her so freshly exciting and shocking that when, more than thirty years later, the therapist asked her about her most vivid memory, what came to mind was none other than the sunlight that had beaten down on the yard that day. The increasing heat on her back and the nape of her neck. The letters she had scratched in the dirt with a stick. The wondrous promise of the phonemes, which had combined so tenuously.

After starting primary school, she began jotting down vocabulary in the back of her diary. With neither purpose nor context, merely a list of words that had made a deep impression on her; among them, the one she valued the most was 숲. On the page, this single-syllable word resembled an old pagoda: ㅍ, the foundation, ㅜ, the main body, ㅅ, the upper section. She liked the feeling when she pronounced it: ㅅ—ㅜ—ㅍ, s–u–p, the sensation of first pursing her lips, and then slowly, carefully releasing the air. And then of the lips closing. A word completed through silence. Entranced by this word in which pronunciation, meaning and form were all wrapped around in stillness, she wrote: 숲. 숲. *Woods.*

And yet, despite her mother's remembering her as "really bright," no one had noticed her through primary and middle school. She wasn't a troublemaker, and her grades were not remarkable. Yes, she did have a few friends, but there was no socializing outside school. The only time she spent in front of the mirror was when she was washing her face; she wasn't excitable like other schoolgirls, and vague longings for romance practically never troubled her. Once the day's lessons were over, she would head to the local library and read a book unrelated to schoolwork, take a few books home with her, curl up under her blanket and fall asleep while reading. The only person who knew that her life was split violently in two was she herself. The words she'd jotted down in the back of her diary wriggled about of their own volition to form unfamiliar sentences. Now and then, words would thrust their way into her sleep like skewers, startling her awake several times a night. She got less and less sleep, was increasingly overwhelmed by sensory stimuli, and sometimes an inexplicable pain burned against her solar plexus like a metal brand.

The most agonizing thing was how horrifyingly distinct the words sounded when she opened her mouth and pushed them out one by one. Even the most nondescript phrase outlined completeness and incompleteness, truth and lies, beauty and ugliness, with the cold clarity of ice. Spun out white as spider's silk from her tongue and by her hand, those sentences were shameful. She wanted to vomit. She wanted to scream.

It first happened in the winter when she'd just turned sixteen. The language that had pricked and confined her like clothing made from a thousand needles abruptly disappeared. Words still reached her ears, but now a thick, dense layer of air buffered the space between her cochleas and brain. Wrapped in that foggy silence, the memories of the tongue and lips that had been used to pronounce, of the hand that had firmly gripped the pencil, grew remote. She no longer thought in language. She moved without language and understood without language—as it had been before she learned to speak, no, before she had obtained life, silence, absorbing the flow of time like balls of cotton, enveloped her body both outside and in.

The psychiatrist, to whom her alarmed mother had taken her, gave her tablets that she hid under her tongue and later buried in the flowerbed at home, and two seasons went by with her squatting in that corner of the yard where she'd long ago got her head around consonants and vowels, soaking up the afternoon sunlight. Before summer arrived, the nape of her neck was already tanned dark, and an angry-looking rash broke out on the base of her nose, which was permanently slick with sweat. By the time dark red stamens began to sprout from the salvia in the flowerbed, nourished by her buried medicine, a consultation between the psychiatrist and her mother resulted in her being sent back to school. It was clear that being cooped up at home hadn't helped, and she mustn't fall behind her peers.

The state high school that she was entering for the first time, months after the letter announcing the new school year beginning in March had arrived at their door, was a dreary, intimidating place. The classes were already far advanced. The teachers were imperious regardless of age. None of her peers showed any interest in a girl who spoke not a single word from morning to evening. When she was called on to read from a textbook or when the students were told to count out loud during PE, she would look vacantly up at the teachers and, without exception, be sent to the back of the classroom or have her cheek slapped.

Despite what her psychiatrist and mother had hoped, the stimulus of social interaction couldn't fracture her silence. Instead a brighter and more concentrated stillness filled the dark clay jar of her body. In the crowded streets on the way home, she walked weightless, as though moving encased in a huge soap bubble. Inside this gleaming quiet, which was like gazing up at the surface from under water, cars roared thunderously by and pedestrians' elbows jabbed her in the shoulders and arms, then vanished.

———————

After a long time had passed, she began to wonder.

What if that perfectly ordinary French word, in that perfectly ordinary lesson, that winter just before the holidays, hadn't sparked something in her? What if she hadn't inadvertently remembered language, like remembering the existence of an atrophied organ?

Why French and not, say, Classical Chinese or English, might have been because of the novelty of it, because it was a language she could opt to learn now that she was in secondary school. Her gaze had lifted blankly to the blackboard as usual, but there it had snagged on something. The short, balding French teacher was pointing to the word as he pronounced it. Caught off guard, she found her lips trembling into motion like a child's. *Bibliothèque.* The mumbled sound came from a place deeper than tongue and throat.

There was no way she could have known how important that moment was.

The terror was still only vague, the pain hesitant to reveal its burning circuit from the depths of silence. Where spelling, phonemes and loose meaning met, a slow-burning fuse of elation and transgression was lit.

·

The woman rests both hands on the desk. Her posture stiff, she bows as though she is a child waiting to have her fingernails examined. She listens to the man's voice filling the lecture room.

"In addition to the passive and the active voice, there is a third voice in Ancient Greek, which I explained briefly in the previous lesson, yes?"

The young man sitting in the same row as the woman nods emphatically. He's a second-year philosophy student, whose rounded cheeks give him the air of a smart, mischievous kid.

The woman turns to look over toward the window. Her gaze passes over the profile of the postgraduate student, who scraped a pass in pre-med but didn't have it in him to be responsible for the lives of others, so gave it up to study the history of medicine. He's big and has a chubby, double-chinned face, round, black, horn-rimmed glasses, and at first glance appears easy-going. He spends every break with the young philosophy student—they bat silly jokes back and forth in ringing voices. But the instant the lesson begins, his attitude changes. Anyone can see how tense he is, terrified of making a mistake.

"This voice, which we call the middle voice, expresses an action that relates to the subject reflexively."

Outside the second-floor window, sporadic points of orange illuminate the bleak low-rise buildings. The young broadleaf trees hide the bare outline of their skinny black branches in the darkness. Her gaze passes silently over the desolate scene, the frightened features of the postgrad student, the pale wrists of the Greek lecturer.

Unlike before, the silence that has now returned after a period of twenty years is neither warm, nor dense, nor bright. If that original silence had been similar to that which exists before birth, this new silence is more like that which follows death. Whereas in the past she had been submerged under water, staring up at the glimmering world above, she now seems to have become a shadow, riding on the cold hard surface of walls and bare ground, an outside observer of a life contained in an enormous water tank. She can hear and read every single word, but her lips won't crack open to emit sound.

Like a shadow bereft of physical form, like the hollow interior of a dead tree, like that dark blank interstitial space between one meteor and another, it is a bitter, thin silence.

Twenty years ago, she had failed to predict that an unfamiliar language, one with little or no resemblance to her mother tongue, would break her own silence. She has chosen to learn Ancient Greek at this private academy because she wants to reclaim language of her own volition. She is almost entirely uninterested in the literature of Homer, Plato and Herodotus, or the literature of the later period, written in demotic Greek, which her fellow students wish to read in the original. Had a lecture course been offered in Burmese or Sanskrit, languages that use an even more unfamiliar script, she would have chosen them instead.

"For example, using the verb 'to buy' in the middle voice, 'I buy X for myself' ultimately means 'I have X.' The verb 'to love' rendered in the middle voice, 'X is loved,' ultimately means X affects me. There is an expression in English, 'He killed himself,' right? Ancient Greek doesn't need to say 'himself'—if we use the middle voice, the same meaning can be expressed in a single word. Like this," the lecturer says, and writes on the blackboard: ἀπήγξατο.

Musing over the letters on the blackboard, she picks up her pencil and writes the word in her notebook. She hasn't come across a language with such intricate rules before. The verbs change their form according to, variously: the subject's case, gender and number; the mood; the tense, of which there are various grades; and the voice, of which there are three distinct types. But it is thanks to these unusually elaborate and meticulous rules that the individual sentences are, in fact, simple and clear. There is no need to specify the subject, or even to keep to a strict word order. This one word—modified to denote that the subject is a singular, third-person male; the tense perfect, meaning it describes something that occurred at some point in the past; and the voice middle—has compressed within it the meaning "He had at one time tried to kill himself."

Around the period her child—the child she had borne eight years ago and for whom she had now been deemed unfit to care—first learned to speak, she had dreamed of a single word in which all human language was encompassed. It was a nightmare so vivid as to leave her back drenched in sweat. One single word, bonded with a tremendous density and gravity. A language that would, the moment someone opened their mouth and pronounced it, explode and expand as all matter had at the universe's beginning. Every time she put her tired, fretful child to bed and drifted into a light sleep herself, she would dream that the immense crystallized mass of all language was being primed like an ice-cold explosive in the center of her hot heart, encased in her pulsing ventricles.

She bites down on that sensation, the mere memory of which is chilling, and writes: ἀπήγξατο.

A language as cold and hard as a pillar of ice.

A language that does not wait to be combined with any other prior to use, a supremely self-sufficient language.

A language that can part the lips only after irrevocably determining causality and manner.

·

The night is disturbed.

The roar of engines from a motorway half a block away makes incisions in her eardrums like countless skate blades on ice.

The lily magnolia, lit by the glow from the street lights, scatters its bruised petals to the winds. She walks past the voluptuous blooms straining the branches and through the spring night air, which is thick with an anticipatory sweetness of crushed petals. She occasionally raises her hands to her face, despite the knowledge that her cheeks are dry.

Passing by the mailbox, which is stuffed full with leaflets and tax notices, she slides the key into the lock of the ground-floor front door, a ponderous, enduring presence next to the cold gleam of the lift.

The flat is filled with traces of the child, things she'd refused to put away, convinced that one more court proceeding would be sufficient to get him back. The low bookcase next to the old velvet sofa is stuffed full of picture books they began reading together when he was two, while various Lego bricks are kept in corrugated-cardboard boxes decorated with animal stickers.

She'd chosen this place many years ago, on the ground floor so her son could play freely. But he had shown no desire to stamp his feet or run about. When she told him it was okay to use the skipping rope in the living room, he asked, "But won't it be noisy for the worms and snails?"

He was small for his age, and delicately built. A scary scene in a book he was reading would raise his temperature past one hundred degrees, and if he was feeling anxious about something he would vomit or get diarrhea. Because he was both the eldest grandson by the first-born son and the only male child on his father's side, because he was not so very young anymore, because her ex-husband unswervingly maintained that she was too highly strung and that this was a bad influence on the boy—the records of the psychiatric treatment she'd received in her teens were presented as evidence—because her income, compared with her husband's—he had recently been promoted to the bank's head office—was both paltry and irregular, the hearing eventually resulted in a comprehensive defeat. Now, since even that meager salary was no longer forthcoming, mounting a further case was impossible.

·

She sits down on the raised step inside her front door without removing her shoes. She puts her bag down beside her, which contains the thick Greek textbook and dictionary, her exercise book and a flat pencil case. She keeps her eyes closed and waits until the yellow sensor light switches off. Once it goes dark, she opens her eyes. She looks at the black furniture hunkered down in the darkness, the black curtain, the black veranda sunk in stillness. Very slowly, she opens her lips, then presses them together.

The lit fuse of the chilly explosive primed in her heart is no more. The interior of her mouth is as empty as the veins through which the blood no longer flows, it is as empty as a lift shaft where the lift has ceased to operate. She wipes her cheeks, dry as ever, with the back of her hand.

If only she'd made a map of the route her tears used to take.

If only she'd used a needle to engrave pinpricks, or even just traces of blood, over the route where the words used to flow.

But, she mutters, from a place deeper than tongue and throat, *that was too terrible a route.*

3

It was the beginning of the summer when I was fifteen.

It was a Sunday night, and the full moon kept on being momentarily veiled by the grey, uneven cloud cover. I was walking along the darkened road, looking up at that full moon, which was like a silver spoon that no amount of polishing will make shine. A moment came when the lunar halo, which was like a mysterious, disquieting code, spread a purple circle over the clouds.

There were at most three bus stops on the road from the house in Suyuri to the crossroads just off the April 19th Revolution Cemetery, but I walked so slowly that it took me an awfully long time. By the time I reached the corner bookshop, the television screens in the display window of the TV and radio store were showing the start of the nine o'clock news. When I entered the shop, the owner, a middle-aged man with broad, flat suspenders over his wrinkled grey shirt, was just getting ready to close up. I asked him to give me five minutes, and hastily scanned the bookshelves for anything that might catch my eye. One of the books I picked up then was none other than the one I'm holding now, a pocketbook translation of Borges's public lectures on Buddhism.

At the time, my impression of Buddhism was entirely gleaned from what I remembered from the Buddha's Birthday Festival I'd attended a fortnight before with my mother and younger sister. That day and night, I had witnessed a spectacle that, all things considered, could be called the most visually stunning of my as-yet short life. Lanterns festooned with petals individually fashioned from reddish-purple Korean paper were swinging in sunlight in the front courtyard of the temple's main hall. To mark the occasion, the temple distributed meals of fairly bland noodles, which we ate in the shade of the zelkova tree, in front of the offering space, before settling down and waiting for it to get dark. When the paper lanterns were eventually lit, I was enraptured, robbed of my senses— the reds and whites of hundreds of hanji lanterns swaying row upon row in the inky darkness, warm candlelight seeping serenely out from inside. "We have to go home now," my mother insisted, but I was rooted to the spot.

On the Sunday morning when my mother announced that our family had to leave Korea in two months' time, why was it that the image of those lanterns came so clearly to my mind? Despite being vaguely aware that whatever impression those lights had made on me was not quite the same as religious awe, that night when I went to buy an elementary German textbook and conversation tape with the generous amount of cash my mother handed me, I greedily clutched the *Sutta-Nipāta, Dharmapada, Hwaeom Sutra Lectures* and *Yeolbangyeong Lectures,* which had brick-pattern covers and were published by Hyeonamsa. I must have cherished some kind of nebulous and superstitious hope that transporting these books halfway around the world to Germany would keep the fate of my family safe.

This slim volume of Borges made its way on to the list because of my pragmatic expectation that, insofar as it had been written by a Westerner, it would act as a very basic primer. At the time, I didn't pay much attention to the photo of him with his eyes half closed, hands clasped in front of his chest as though praying or regretting, reproduced in black and white on the upper section of the green cover.

I read those books slowly and repeatedly during the seventeen years I spent in Germany. Some nights, wanting nothing more than to run my eyes over the familiar contours of Hangul, I would sit a good long while with an open book and not turn a single page. Whichever book I opened, I could feel again the cool air of that early-summer night in Suyuri. It was down to those books that I managed not to forget the moon that had been like a tarnished silver spoon, its purple halo that had seemed a mysterious premonition of some unsettling happening.

And so the book that ended up being my favorite was the *Hwaeom Sutra Lectures* from Hyeonamsa; never again, in any of the books I subsequently read, did I encounter a system of thought constructed through such dazzling images. Whereas Borges's book was, as I'd expected, easy and general, so I'd flicked through it relatively quickly and then put it aside. Sometime later, when I went to university, I had to read his fiction and a critical biography in German; it was then that I opened this book again and read it with a fresh perspective.

This morning, recalling once more this slim green book, I fetched it from my suitcase in the storeroom. Turning the pages, I discovered a note written in a rough hand. Scribbled directly below a sentence by Borges, *The world is an illusion, and living is dreaming,* it read: *How is that dream so vivid? How does blood flow and hot tears gush forth?*

Below that, I could make out *Life, life* traced in German, then struck out with a thick horizontal line.

It was clearly my hand, and yet I had no memory of having written it. All I knew was that it was the same dark blue ink that German students use for note-taking.

I opened the desk drawer and rummaged around for my old grey leather pencil case. Inside there was a fountain pen, just as I remembered. It was the same pen I'd used when I first moved to Germany; I'd replaced the nib countless times until I finally laid the pen aside during my second year of university. I took off the top, which was intact apart from a few scratches, and carried the fountain pen to the bathroom, to wash away the dried ink crusted on the nib. I filled the sink with clean water and submerged the nib. The dark blue ink ribboned steadily through the water in a slender, wavering line.

4

μὴ ἐρώτησης μηδέν αὐτόν
Do not ask him anything.

μὴ ἄλλως ποιήσης
Do not do it another way.

She sits without speaking amid the loud rumble of the students reading. The Greek lecturer no longer makes an issue of her silence. He angles his body away from the class and wipes the sentences from the blackboard, rubbing the soft eraser cloth over the board with expansive sweeps of his arm.

The students are quiet until he's done. The thin middle-aged man sitting behind the pillar stretches his back and thumps his fist against his vertebrae. The philosophy student moves his index finger over the screen of his smartphone, which he keeps by him on the desk. The postgrad stares at the sentences that are being vigorously erased from the blackboard. His lips part, their thinness in stark contrast to his bulk, and he reads the disappearing words to himself, his voice inaudible.

"Starting in June, we will read Plato," the Greek lecturer announces, leaning his upper body against the now-clean blackboard. "Of course, we will continue to study grammar alongside." He holds the chalk in his right hand, and so uses his left to push his glasses further up his nose.

"Once human beings moved from communicating in silence and only through unsegmented vocal expressions, such as ooh-ooh, to creating the first few words, language gradually acquired a system. By the time this system arrived at its zenith, language had extremely elaborate and complex rules. And that, you see, is precisely the difficulty in learning an ancient language."

He chalks a parabola on the blackboard. The curve rises from the left-hand side in a steep inclination, before sloping off to the right in a long, gentle fall. He taps his index finger on the curve's peak and continues to speak.

"From precisely the moment that it arrives at the zenith, language describes a slow, gentle arc, undergoing alterations that make it a little more convenient to use. In some senses this is decline, this is corruption, but in other aspects it can be called progress. The European languages of today have passed through that long process, becoming less strict, less elaborate, less complicated. When reading Plato, one is able to appreciate the beauty of an ancient language that had arrived at its acme many thousands of years ago."

He does not immediately resume his train of thought, but is silent. The middle-aged man behind the pillar covers his mouth with his fist and gives a short, low cough. When he hems again, this time at length, the young philosophy student gives him a sidelong glance.

"In a manner of speaking, the Greek that Plato used was like a fully ripe fruit about to fall to earth. The sun rapidly set on the Middle Greek that was spoken by the generations that followed him. And, along with their language, the Greek states too fell into decay. And so Plato represents one who stood and watched the sun set not only on language but on everything that surrounded him."

She tries to listen attentively, but is unable to concentrate on each word. That one sentence sticks in her ears, like a long fish cut into pieces, its postpositions and word endings not yet scaled. *In silence. Unsegmented vocal expressions. Uh-uh, ooh-ooh. The first few words.*

Before she lost words—when she was still able to use them to write—she sometimes wished that her own expressions would more closely resemble inarticulacy: a moan or low cry. The sound of suffering through bated breath. Snarling. Humming in one's half-sleep to pacify a child. Stifled laughter. The sound of two people's lips pressing together, pulling apart.

There had been times when she had peered at the shapes of the words she'd just written, before slowly opening her lips and sounding them out. She had at once been struck by the incongruity of the flattened forms that resembled pinned-down bodies and her own voice belatedly attempting to speak them. She would stop reading and swallow, her throat dry. Like those times when she had to immediately press down on a cut to stop the bleeding, or, on the contrary, to strain to squeeze out blood and prevent bacteria from entering her bloodstream.

5.

Voice

If you're reading this letter now—if it wasn't returned to me unopened—your family will still be living on the first floor of the hospital, back in Germany.

The stone building, said to have been built as a printing house in the eighteenth century, would by now be covered in pale ivy. Tiny violets would have bloomed and faded in the cracks between the stone steps leading down to the courtyard. The dandelions would have withered, leaving only a crown of pale ghost-like seeds. The wild ants would be marching up and down the steps in regimented lines, looking like thick punctuation marks.

Is your mother still as beautiful as ever, still wearing those gorgeously patterned saris I always saw her in, a different color every time? And is your father, elderly now, whose cold, grey eyes used to examine my own, still working as an ophthalmologist? And your daughter, how old is she now? As you read this letter, are you back at your parents' for a visit, giving them a few days to dote on their granddaughter? Are you staying in the north-facing room that was yours as a child, do you go for walks by the river, pushing the pram in front of you? Do you sit and rest on the bench you always liked, the one in front of the old bridge, take out some photographic negatives, which you always used to carry around in your pockets, and hold them up to the sun?

The first time I sat with you, side by side on that bench in front of the bridge, you reached into the pocket of your jeans and brought out two negatives, remember? You raised your slim, dark arms, held the film in front of your eyes and looked up at the sun.

My heart pounded unbearably—because I had seen you make the same gesture before.

It was the day of my first appointment with your father, one afternoon early in June. On a metal bench in the hospital courtyard where the lilacs were in full bloom, your black hair tumbling loose on to your shoulders, you were sitting and looking at the sun through pieces of film. The male nurse with the curt expression, who had been sitting next to you, gestured for you to give him one of them. There was something amusing in the sight of two fully grown people sitting side by side and each squinting up at the sun through a piece of film.

Unaware of my presence, concealed as I was behind the shaded glass door, the man looked away from the film and said a few words to you. You watched his lips move with a look of deep concentration. Just then, he leaned forward and planted a quick, awkward kiss on your mouth. This surprised me, as it was obvious even to a casual observer that the two of you weren't intimate. And it seemed that you were equally shocked, because you recoiled, but then gave him a swift peck on the cheek, as if to say that you forgave him. As if this were part of the generous etiquette of the friendship that had sprung up between you as you sat and looked at the sun together. You lightly got to your feet and took the film from the man's hand. He laughed awkwardly, his face burning. You laughed too. Still looking embarrassed, he sat and stared after you as you turned round and disappeared without a word.

Of course, you couldn't have known what a deep impression those few minutes of perfect stillness made on my seventeen-year-old self. Not long after, I learned that you were the daughter of the hospital's owner, that as a newborn you had contracted a fever and lost your hearing, that after graduating from a special-education school two years ago you now passed your time making wooden furniture in a workshop at the rear of the hospital. Yet this string of facts could not fully explain the chill I'd felt witnessing that brief scene.

Afterward, every time I stepped through the hospital's main door when I had an appointment, every time I heard the buzz of the power saw coming from your workshop, every time I saw you from far off strolling casually along the banks of the river, dressed in work clothes, my mind would go blank as though I had suddenly inhaled the scent of lilacs. A tremor would pass through my lips, which had never yet known another's, like a tiny electric shock.

In looks, you took after your mother.

Your deep brown skin and black hair, which you usually wore tied up, were both attractive, but the most beautiful thing about you was your eyes. The eyes of a person well used to solitary labor. Eyes that were a soft mixture of earnestness and mischievousness, warmth and sadness. Dark eyes that moved gently over their object, never straining, taking in what they saw without leaping to any hasty judgments.

Now would have been the moment to place a hand on your shoulder and ask for one of the negatives, but I couldn't bring myself to do it. Waiting for you to take your eyes from the film, I contented myself with staring at your round forehead, at the strands of curly hair clinging to your skin, at the ridge of your nose that seemed to be wanting a small jewel, and at the round beads of sweat that had formed there.

"What can you see?"

You watched my lips intently as I asked the question. In that moment, I found myself able to understand the stern-faced male nurse. I knew you were simply trying to read my lips, but, even so, I was struck by a sudden desire to kiss you. You brought out a notebook from the front pocket of your loose work shirt and wrote in it with a ballpoint pen.

See for yourself.

At that point, my vision was already fading. Your father explained his medical opinion that a premature operation would only serve to hasten blindness; he spoke slowly and carefully and kept his face deliberately impassive, refusing to betray any cheap sympathy.

That strong light was harmful had not yet been proved, but he advised caution all the same, stressing that it was always best to be on the safe side. He advised me to wear sunglasses during the daytime, when the sun's rays were at their strongest, and to have only dim lighting on at night. Constantly going around in dark sunglasses like some celebrity made me feel self-conscious, so I chose a pair of glasses with pale green lenses for everyday use. Given all this, looking directly at the sun was something I couldn't contemplate, however much I used film as a medium.

Aware of my hesitation, you wrote in the notebook again: *Later.* Your hand was deft and exact; presumably, you were well used to written conversations. *Just before it gets to the point where you can't see anything at all.*

Only then did I realize that you were fully aware of my prognosis. The idea of your family discussing my condition around the dinner table wounded me deeply, though it existed only in my imagination.

I was silent. Having given up waiting for an answer, you closed the notebook and put it back in your pocket.

We watched the river.

As if that were all that was permitted.

An unfamiliar sadness came over me, which I instantly understood was due neither to the hurt I had just received nor to the sense of having been affronted. Still less was it down to fear or dismay over what the days ahead might bring. The time when I would no longer be able to see anything at all was still far in the future. This sadness, both bitter and sweet, was something that stemmed from your earnest face in profile, unbelievably close to my own at that moment; from your lips, which seemed to hold a barely perceptible electric current; from your black pupils, so very clear.

That moment when the river water scintillated in the July sunlight like the scales of a huge fish, when you suddenly placed your hand on my arm, when I trembled to touch the dark blue veins running raised over the back of your hand, when, gripped by fear, I finally brought my lips to yours—has that moment now disappeared inside you? In front of that old bridge, does your daughter peek out from the pram and say, "Mama," and do you put the film strip back in your pocket and slowly stand up?

More than twenty years have swept by, but certain aspects of that moment have not gone from my memory. Not only that moment alone, but all the moments we spent together—yes, even the most awful—are wholly alive for me. That which pains me even more than my self-accusation, my regret, is your face. That face, a mask of tears. The fist that slammed into my own face, harder than a man's, having spent so many years handling wood.

Will you forgive me?

And if you are unable to forgive me, will you at least remember that I seek it of you?

·

I'm approaching forty, which your father warned would be the cut-off point, but I retain partial sight. Perhaps in another year or so I will be totally blind. It's been a long, slow process, and by now I need no further preparations. Like a prisoner taking one last drawn-out drag on the single cigarette he's been allowed, on bright days I pass the long afternoons sitting in the alleyway in front of the house, drinking in the scene.

People from all walks of life pass through this alley, in a shopping district on the outskirts of Seoul. A teenage girl wearing earphones, her school skirt clumsily hitched up. A middle-aged man with a shabby tracksuit and a paunch. A woman talking on her mobile whose stunning dress makes her look as though she'd just stepped from the pages of a fashion magazine. An elderly woman, with her white hair cropped short and a sparklingly embellished sweater, leisurely lighting her cigarette. Someone somewhere is swearing viciously, and the smell of gukbap wafts from a restaurant. A kid on a bike whooshes past me, ringing the bell as loudly as he can.

Even wearing glasses with the highest power I could get, I still can't make out the details of any of these things. Individual shapes and gestures blur together, and any clarity is brought about only through the strength of my imagination. The schoolgirl will be mouthing the words to the song she's listening to, and her lower lip will have a small, bluish mark on the left, just as yours did. The middle-aged man's tracksuit sleeves will be grubby and worn to a shine, and the laces in his sneakers, which would originally have been white, would have turned a dark grey from months of not being washed. Beads of sweat will be trickling down the temples of the boy on the bike. The old woman looks like quite a tough proposition; her cigarette will be some slender, dainty brand, and the twinkling shards of mother-of-pearl encrusted on her sweater will form the shape of a rose or hydrangea.

When people-watching and its attendant flights of fancy become tedious, I slowly walk up the path that leads to the mountain. The pale green trees undulate as a single mass, their flowers a riot of unbelievably beautiful colors. When I come to the small temple at the foot of the mountain, I sit and rest on the wooden maru outside the public hall. I remove my heavy glasses and gaze at the world's now-faint contours. It's a common belief that blind or partially sighted people will pick up on sounds first and foremost, but that isn't the case with me. The first thing I perceive is time. I sense it as a slow, cruel current of enormous mass passing constantly through my body to gradually overcome me.

Because my vision worsens rapidly as the light fades, I can't allow myself to stay sitting here for too long. I go home, change my clothes, wash my face. I have to go to teach my students, you see— the class starts at seven in the evening, which is your noon, the time when you best liked to look up at the sun. I generally arrive at the private academy when it's still light, then wait until seven. Inside the brightly lit building my movements are largely unimpeded, but, even with my glasses on, walking alone through the streets at night is a burden. Around ten, when the class finishes and the students all file out, I order a taxi to the academy entrance to bring me home.

What do I teach at the academy?

On Mondays and Thursdays I teach elementary Ancient Greek, and on Fridays an intermediate class reading Plato in the original. Each class has no more than eight students. They're a mix of university students with an interest in Western philosophy, and others of varying age and backgrounds.

Whatever their motivation, those who study Greek share certain tendencies. They walk and talk slowly, for the most part, and don't show much emotion (I guess this applies to me too). Perhaps because this language is a long-dead one and doesn't allow for oral communication. Silence, shy hesitation and reactions of muted laughter slowly heat the air inside the classroom, and slowly cool it.

And so the days go by here, without incident.

Even the occasional memorable event is soon erased without a trace under time's huge, opaque mass.

The year I first left Korea and went to Germany, I was fifteen. Since I was thirty-two by the time I made the return trip, my life at that point had been cloven into two almost exact halves, split between two languages, two cultures. I had to choose one of these two as the place where I would live once I turned forty, with all the changes your father had warned me that time would bring. When I said that I wanted to return to where I could use my mother tongue, everyone around me, including my family and my teachers, tried to dissuade me. My mother and younger sister both asked me what I planned to do back in the mother country. My degree in Ancient Greek philosophy, so difficult to obtain, would be worthless there, they said, not to mention how I'd need my family given my situation—I couldn't do it alone. It was only with great difficulty that I managed to persuade them to agree to my plan of spending two years alone as a trial period.

I've been here for three times those initial two years now, and still haven't come to a decision. After that first autumn that I spent marveling at, and moved by, my mother tongue, which I had missed unbearably, winter came crashing in from all directions like a landslide, and Seoul began to seem more like a stranger to me, just as the German cities had once seemed. Shoulders hunched inside their colorless woolen coats and sweaters, people brushed past me with faces that spoke of long endurance, and even longer endurance yet to come, as they hurried along the frozen streets. Just as I had done in Germany, I looked on, an expressionless observer.

And so here I am, having managed to avoid succumbing to sentimentality or optimism. The small talk I exchange with the unusually shy students, the fastidious principal of the humanities academy, who somehow makes a profit by hiring a handful of "star" lecturers and keeps things afloat, and the part-time admin with the bobbed hair whose hay fever means she can never afford to be without tissues, whatever the season, provides me with some quiet enjoyment as I pass my days here. In the mornings, I use a magnifying glass to go over the sentences we will read in class that day and commit them to memory; I muse over the fuzzy reflection of my face in the mirror above the washbasin, and stroll leisurely through bright streets and alleyways when the mood takes me. There are times when my eyes burn and suddenly start to water. When these tears, which are but physiological, fail to stop for some reason, I quietly turn away from the road and wait for the moment to pass.

•

Is the sunlight full on your tanned face now as you turn and push the pram back the way you came? Does a bundle of bushy foxtail that you picked sway gently from your two-year-old daughter's clasped hand? Instead of taking the direct route home from the river, do you stop in front of that ancient cathedral? Do you lift up the baby with your two strong arms, leave the pram with the warden and step into the cool of the cathedral's interior?

A place where the seemingly ice-steeped sunlight streams in through stained-glass windows in various gradations of blue. A place where Christ hangs on the cross without the slightest trace of suffering, his eyes lifted ingenuously toward heaven, and the angels step lightly through the air as though out for a casual stroll. Palm trees with dark and still-darker green leaves sweetly unfurled.

Bright-faced saints with pale blue-grey hair draped in paler blue-grey vestments. A space without a hint of sin or suffering, and which for that reason I'd felt was almost pagan: the church of St. Stephan.

The late-summer evening all those years ago, when we walked there together, side by side, you wrote something in your notebook and showed it to me. You said that you'd grown up with a deep religious faith, but that, however much you tried, you couldn't believe in the existence of anything as extreme as heaven and hell. Instead, it seemed to you that spirits were real and wandered the darkened streets into the early morning. And if such spirits existed, then surely God must also exist, somewhere. I found it amusing that the foundation of the belief you claimed in the Christian God was not only illogical but entirely un-Christian and, laughing out loud, took your notebook. I jotted down a demonstration of God's non-existence that I'd read somewhere, and handed it back to you.

There is evil in this world, and it causes the suffering of innocent people.

If God is good but unable to redress this, he is impotent.

If God is not good and merely omnipotent, and does not redress these things, he is evil.

If God is neither good nor omnipotent, he cannot be called God.

Therefore the real existence of a good and omnipotent God is an impossible fallacy.

Your eyes widen when you are genuinely angry. Your thick brows rise, your lashes and lips quiver, and your chest heaves with every breath you gasp. As soon as I returned the pen, you hastily scrawled in the notebook:

In that case my God is both good and full of sorrow. If you are at-
tracted to such nonsensical arguments, one day your own real existence
will become an impossible fallacy.

.

Sometimes I put the question to myself using the form of Greek logic you so detested. When we take as true the premise that if something is lost, something else is gained, given that I lost you, what have I gained? What will I now gain through the loss of the visible world?

There is, inevitably, something tenuous and unsatisfactory in the way the logical demonstration works, sifting all humankind's sufferings and regrets, attachments, sadness, and weaknesses through the loose net of truth and falsity to obtain a handful of premises like a handful of gold dust. Boldly casting fallacies aside and proceeding along the narrow balance beam one step at a time, we see silence rippling like a black body of water past the net of clear, coherent questions we've asked and answered ourselves. And still we go on asking and answering—even as our eyes remain immersed in the silence, in the menacing blue quiet that is constantly rising, like the black water. Why had I been such a fool when it came to loving you? My love for you wasn't foolish, but I was; had my own innate foolishness made love itself foolish? Or is it that I myself wasn't all that foolish, but love's inherent foolishness awakened any foolishness latent in me and eventually smashed everything to pieces?

τὴν ἀμαθίαν καταλύεται ἡ ἀλήθεια.

This sentence, written in the middle voice, states that truth destroys foolishness. Is this true? When truth destroys foolishness, is truth necessarily altered by the encounter, influenced by the very thing it has destroyed? Does a fissure form in foolishness when it destroys truth? When my foolishness destroyed love, if I claim that that foolishness was equally undone in the process, would you call that sophistry? Voice. Your voice. The sound I have not forgotten in more than twenty years. If I said that I still loved that voice, would you slam your fist into my face again?

·

In the lip-reading class at the special-ed school that you'd attended for over a decade, you told me you learned to read lips and to speak German. One night not long after we'd had this written conversation, it occurred to me: what would it be like to hear you speak, as you'd learned to do in that class?

That summer, unbeknownst to my family, I'd bought a German Sign Language textbook and was spending every night practicing the phrases. I used my own reflection in the small mirror by the desk to practice, and an hour or so of this was enough to leave my back and armpits soaked with sweat. But it wasn't difficult or boring, not in the slightest. In fact, those nights were filled with a sweetness I know I will never experience again. It was around then that I realized for the first time that falling in love is like being haunted. Even before I opened my eyes in the morning, you would slip in under my eyelids. When I opened them, you instantly transferred to the ceiling, the wardrobe, the windowpane, the street, the far-off sky, and glimmered there like dappled light. You haunted me more persistently than I imagine any ghost ever could. In the small mirror by the desk that summer night, what was reflected was the upper half of my body as I sweated through my clumsy gestures and signs and facial expressions, but I recognized the glow of your face shimmering over mine at every moment.

You speak to me.

That night, I mumbled this sentence, which first came to me in German, out loud in my mother tongue.

This immediately brought up an image: the pile of freshly cut timber in your workshop. Making sure that nobody saw me—I was particularly anxious not to have your father find out about it—I would hide myself there, among the timber, and watch you work. I never tired of watching you as you sawed, planed and sanded planks of wood. If it was a big job, I would have time to become intimately acquainted with every nook and cranny of your workshop. I would put my nose to, or run my fingers along, the planks you'd stacked against one wall to dry. Fragrant cryptomeria. White fir. Pine, which gave off a subtle scent from up close. Woody growth rings resembling the arc of your shoulders.

At the time, I vaguely imagined that your voice might resemble the feel and scent of that timber.

But curiosity and musings weren't the reason I was interested in hearing your voice, not at all. I was seventeen at the time, and you were my first love. I was convinced I wanted to live with you. I believed we would remain together for as long as we had life in us. And this scared me. I knew I was going blind. Eventually I wouldn't be able to see you. Eventually I wouldn't be able to converse with you, whether through writing or by signing.

A few weeks later, on a weekend afternoon when the weather

suddenly took a turn and you were taking a break and making tea, I asked you a question. Carefully, unaware of any danger. No, with the innocence of ignorance.

"Could you say something, anything, to me, like you learned in your lip-reading class?"

You watched my lips intently, then met my eyes with a dazed look. And so I explained. That at some point we would live together, and that I would go blind. That when I was unable to see, we would need spoken words.

You couldn't have known how often I longed to turn back time, how much I wanted to take back those foolish words. Your face turned cold and hard and you threw me out of the workshop, where the scent of the wood had been intensified by the drizzle. You wouldn't see me anymore, of course wouldn't kiss me, wouldn't let me bury my face in your long black hair, the sweetly scented nape of your neck, or your delicate collarbone, wouldn't let me slide my ardent hand under your shirt to feel your heartbeat, steadfastly refused to see me even when I loitered in front of your house from the early hours, slammed the workshop door shut whether my fingers got caught or not, and eventually, one night a few weeks later, punched my frantically beseeching face.

We were both of us stunned. Without picking up my glasses, which had been knocked to the floor, leaving the faintly sweet-tasting blood to run down from my nose and lips, I clutched your leg. Shaking, you shoved me to the ground. Eyes blazing, you suddenly opened your mouth.

"Out, now!"

That voice.

The sound of the wind scratching and whistling through crannies in the window frame on a winter's night. The sound of a fretsaw screeching over iron, of splintering glass. Your voice.

I crawled forward on my belly and clutched your leg again. Did you really not know? I loved you. When, in some incomprehensible paroxysm, you picked up a piece of wood and used it to hit me in the face, when I fainted right then and there, did you see, did you notice the burning tears streaming from my eyes?

.

Since foolishness destroyed that period of my life and itself along with it, I know now that, had we in fact lived together, I wouldn't have needed your voice after I went blind. For even as the visible world would gradually have receded like an ebb tide, at the same time, the silence we shared would have gradually become replete.

Several years after I lost you, I did look at the sun through two pieces of film. At six in the evening, though, not at noon; I was too afraid for that. My eyes burned as though a thin acid had been poured into them, and I couldn't hold on for long. Nor did I manage to learn what had so fascinated you. Only: I yearned for you. For the back of your hand, no longer by my side. For the deep blue veins raised up under your skin.

.

Now do you hold your child in your arms as you step out of the dark cathedral?

Do you get the pram back from the warden, install your child in it and buckle her in? Do you secure the stray strands of your hair, then set off home? Do you walk through those same streets where my seventeen-year-old self paced restlessly to and fro, from early dawn, full of foolishness and agony, along the black cobblestoned pavement? Every time the wheels of the pram are jolted upward, do you lay your hand on the child's chest to soothe her? Do you walk on, taking step after soundless step, with your God, whom goodness makes sorrowful, on your shoulder?

The sun rises seven hours later where you are than it does here.

On a day not so far away now, I'll be holding up pieces of film under the noon sun, and you'll be asleep in the darkness of five o'clock in the morning. A deep blue light like that of the veins on the back of your hand will not have entirely leached from the sky. Your heart will beat the regular beat of sleep, and now and again your eyes, which had burned and blurred with tears, will flutter beneath their lids. When I walk into complete darkness, is it all right if I remember you without this unrelenting ache?

6

παῦσαι.	μὴ παύσῃ.
Stop.	Don't stop.
ἐρώτηόον με.	μὴ ἐρώτησῃς μηδέν αὐτόν.
Ask me.	Don't ask me anything.
ἄλλως ποίησον.	μὴ ποίησῃς μηδαμῶς/ἄλλως
Do [it] another way.	Do not do [it] another way at all.

After filling the dark green blackboard with sentences, the man stands to one side and leans his upper body against it. He doesn't realize that the shoulders of his dark blue shirt are covered with a dusting of white chalk. His clean-shaven face is very pale, which makes him look unexpectedly young; one could almost mistake him for a graduate student, if it weren't for his sunken cheeks. Fine wrinkles announcing the muted beginnings of aging cluster visibly around his eyes and mouth.

7

Eyes

Even when she could talk, she'd always been soft-spoken.

It wasn't an issue of vocal cords or lung capacity. She just didn't like taking up space. Everyone occupies a certain amount of physical space according to their body mass, but voice travels far beyond that. She had no wish to disseminate her self.

Whether on the subway or in the street, in a café or restaurant, she never spoke in an unreservedly loud voice or called out after someone to get their attention. In every situation—the only exception was when she was lecturing—hers was the quietest voice in the room. Already very thin, she would hunch her shoulders and back so that her body took up less room. She understood humor and had quite a cheerful smile, but when she laughed it was so low as to be barely audible.

The grey-haired therapist pointed this out to her. Going by the book, he tried to find the root cause in her childhood. She cooperated with him only halfway. Not wishing to disclose her experience of having lost language as a preteen, she managed to retrieve a memory from further back.

Her mother had come down with what appeared to be typhoid fever when she was pregnant with her. Suffering alternate bouts of fever and chills, she took a handful of tablets with every meal for about a month. Her mother had been brash and impetuous by nature, quite unlike her daughter, and as soon as she was back on her feet she went to the gynecologist and said she wanted the baby gone. She had determined that it couldn't possibly turn out healthy, given the medication she'd been taking.

The doctor told her that a termination would be dangerous, as the placenta had already formed, and told her to come back in two months' time, when he would give her an injection to induce a stillbirth. But when those two months were almost over and the fetus began to move, her resolve weakened, and she did not go to the hospital. She was plagued by anxiety up until the moment the baby was born. Only after repeatedly counting the newborn baby's fingers and toes, still slick with amniotic fluid, was her mind set at ease.

Aunts, cousins, even the meddling neighbor who lived next door, told this anecdote to her while she was growing up. *You came within an inch of not being born.* That sentence was repeated like an incantation.

She was too young to be able to read her own emotions well, but the horrifying coldness contained in that sentence was something she felt clearly. She almost hadn't been born. The world was not something that had been given to her as a matter of course. It was merely a possibility that the chance combination of countless variables in the pitch-blackness had permitted, a fragile bubble that had coalesced ever so briefly in the nick of time. One evening, after saying an awkward goodbye to her mother's boisterous, cheerful guests, she had squatted on the maru at the front of the house and watched as the gathering twilight buried the yard. She told the therapist how, as she sat there with muffled breath and huddled shoulders, she had felt the thin, flimsy, enormous single-layer world being swallowed up in the darkness.

The therapist thought this was all very interesting. After she'd replied in the negative to his question of whether this might be her earliest memory, she rummaged through her thoughts a little further and produced for him the memory of the day she'd spent in the sun-beaten yard—when she'd first become aware of the phonemes of her mother tongue. The therapist was greatly taken by the anecdote and attempted to form a conclusion from a careful combination of the two memories.

"That you were so enraptured by language as to recall it as your earliest memory—isn't this because you were instinctively aware that the circuit connecting language to the world is something that only just holds together, something in constant danger of failing? In other words, unconsciously, did you find that fascination to be somehow similar to your sense of the world's contingency?" The therapist studied her face. "Now tell me, do you perhaps remember the first dream you ever had?"

Struck by the stray thought that he might be planning to include her as a case study in one of his books, she suddenly became uneasy and didn't respond. She didn't disclose to him the dream she'd had not long after she'd taught herself to read, a dream that had been strangely vivid and cold. In the dream snow was falling in an unfamiliar street somewhere, as adults with expressionless faces brushed past her. She stood, a child alone by the roadside, wearing unfamiliar clothes. That was all. Nothing happened, and nothing was concluded. There was only the cold; the snowy road silent as though her ears were muffled; people she had never seen before; and her own body, standing, alone.

While she remained silent, struggling to concentrate on the details of the dream, the therapist proceeded toward a prescription. "You were too young to understand life, and naturally were without the means to live independently then, and every time you heard about what a close call your birth had been, you felt a sense of being threatened, as though your whole existence were going to be blotted out. But you've grown into a fine adult and now are strong enough to face such things. You don't have to be afraid. You don't have to cower. It's all right to speak up. Straighten your shoulders and take up as much space as you like."

But she knew that if she followed that reasoning the rest of her life would be one long struggle to find a response to the question that constantly threatened to destroy her fragile equilibrium—the question of whether she really had any claim to existence. Something in the therapist's lucid, beautiful conclusion didn't sit right. She still did not wish to take up more space, nor did she believe that she had lived in thrall to fear, or spent her life suppressing what came naturally to her.

Their sessions progressed smoothly, and so when after five months her voice hadn't grown stronger and instead she became mute, the therapist seemed genuinely shocked. "I understand," he said. "I understand how much you've suffered. It must have been agonizing for you to accept losing the custody battle, not to mention the death of your mother immediately before. How unbearably you must have missed your child in the last few months. I understand. You must have felt that it was impossible to withstand everything on your own."

The exaggerated note of earnest sympathy in his voice astounded her. What she found most intolerable was his claim that he understood her. This was simply not true, and she knew it with a serene certainty.

Silence, the quiet assuager, enveloped them, waiting.

She picked up the pen and paper in front of her and wrote in a neat hand: *No. It isn't that simple.*

·

When she was still speaking, she would sometimes simply fix her eyes on her interlocutor, as though she believed it was possible to translate perfectly what she wished to say through her gaze. She greeted people, expressed thanks and apologized, all with her eyes rather than words. To her, there was no touch as instantaneous and intuitive as the gaze. It was close to being the only way of touching without touch.

Language, by comparison, is an infinitely more physical way to touch. It moves lungs and throat and tongue and lips, it vibrates the air as it wings its way to the listener. The tongue grows dry, saliva spatters, the lips crack. When she found that physical process too much to bear, she became paradoxically more verbose. She would spin out long, intricate sentences, shunning the vitality and fluidity of easy conversation. Her voice would be louder than usual. The more people paid attention to what she was saying, the more abstract her speech became and the more broadly she smiled. When these instances recurred at frequent intervals, she found she was unable to concentrate on writing, even when she was alone.

In the periods directly before she lost speech, she became a greater talker than ever. And she was unable to write for increasingly longer stretches. Just as she had always disliked the way her voice diffused through the air, she found it difficult to tolerate the disturbance her sentences wreaked on the silence. At times, she could taste bile at the back of her throat even before she put pen to paper, merely by thinking about arranging a word or two.

But that couldn't be the cause of her muteness either. *It couldn't be that simple.*

·

δύσβατός γέ τις ὁ τόπος
φαίνεται καὶ ἐπίσκιος.
ἔστι γοῦν σκοτεινὸς καὶ
δυσδιερεύνητος.

This place is a place
where it is difficult to take a step in any given direction.
All around has grown dark
It is a place where it is difficult to find anything.

She bends her head over the book that lies open on her desk. It's a thick dual-language edition of the first few books of *The Republic*, containing both the original Greek and the Korean translation. Drops of sweat trickle down from her temples and fall on to the

Greek sentences. The coarse-grained recycled paper bulges where they land.

When she raises her head, it seems as though the dimly lit classroom has suddenly brightened, unsettling her. Only then does she properly pick up on the hushed conversation that the usually quiet man behind the pillar is conducting with the postgrad.

"Angkor Wat. I got back from there yesterday morning. Four nights, five days; an early-summer holiday. I was tired from the flight and thought I might skip class today, but it seemed a waste of tuition to skip two weeks in a row. Ha, ha, I'm still pretty fit, you know. Go hiking every weekend. Hmm, I can't tell, but people have been saying I look tanned. Ah, you can't compare the heat out there to how it is here. They have a squall at least once every day, but it barely takes the edge off the heat . . . It's just, you know, I'm interested in ruins. There was ancient Khmer writing engraved on the temple stones and I liked the look of it more than the Ancient Greek script."

She looks up at the blackboard, blank now during the break. The lecturer has wiped it clean with the cloth eraser, but only lightly, so there are still the odd fragments of Greek script visible. She can even make out one third of a sentence. And a rough whirl of smudged chalk that looks intentional, like it was done with a broad brush.

She bends over the book again. She takes in a deep breath, and hears the distinct sound of her inhalation. Since losing speech, she gets the sense sometimes that her inhales and exhales resemble speech. They seem to stir the silence as boldly as the voice does.

She'd had a similar thought while witnessing her mother's final moments. Every time her mother, by then in a coma, expelled a mouthful of hot breath, silence had taken a step back. And when she breathed in, the shudderingly cold silence had shrieked as it was sucked into her mother's body.

She clutches the pencil and peers at the sentence she was just reading. She could puncture every single one of these letters. If she pressed down with the pencil lead and made a long tear, she could bore through a whole word, no, a whole sentence. She examines the small black letters, conspicuous on the coarse grey paper, the diacritics that resemble insects both curled up and stretching their backs. A place in shadow, obscured and difficult to tread. A sentence in which Plato, no longer young, ponders and stalls for time. The indistinct voice of someone whose mouth is hidden behind their hand.

She tightens her grip on the pencil. Carefully, she breathes out. The emotion permeating the sentence becomes apparent, like chalk marks or a casual thread of dried blood. She endures it.

.

Her body bears witness to the fact of her long-term muteness. It appears firmer or heavier than it really is. Her footsteps, the movements of her hands and arms, the long, rounded contours of her face and shoulders—all demarcate clear, strong perimeters. Nothing seeps out, and nothing seeps in past these limits.

She'd never been one to spend a great deal of time examining herself in the mirror, but now the very thought seems incomprehensible to her. The face we each imagine most frequently over the course of our lives must be our own. But once she stopped picturing her face, she found that over time it began to feel unreal. When she happens to catch a glimpse of her face reflected in a window or mirror, she examines her eyes carefully. Those two clear pupils seem to her to be the only passage linking her to that stranger's face.

Sometimes she thinks of herself as more like some form of substance, a moving solid or liquid, than like a person. When she eats hot rice, she feels that she herself becomes that rice, and when she washes her face with cold water there is no distinction between her and that water. At the same time she knows that she is neither rice nor water, but some harsh, solid substance that will never commingle with any being, living or otherwise. The only things that she sees as worth reclaiming from the icy silence, something that takes all the strength she possesses, are the face of the child with whom she has been allowed to spend one night every two weeks, and the dead Greek words that she gouges into the paper with the pencil she grips.

γῆ κεῖται γυνή.
A woman lies on the ground.

She puts down the pencil, which is sticky with sweat. With the palm of her hand, she wipes away the beads of moisture that cling to her temples.

·

"Mum, they've said I can't come here any more after September."

Last Saturday night, she had stared at her son's face in alarm at these words. He'd grown again, even in the space of two weeks, looking taller, but also slimmer, than before. His lashes were long and thin, tiny diagonals clearly outlined over his soft white cheeks, like a miniature drawing done in pen.

"I don't want to go. My English isn't even that good. Dad's sister who lives there, I've never even met her. He says I have to go for a whole year. I've only just managed to make friends, and now I have to move again?"

She'd just bathed and put the child to bed, and an apple scent rose from his hair. She could see her face reflected in his round eyes. His face was reflected again in the reflection of her eyes, and in those eyes there was her face again . . . in an infinite series of reflections.

"Mum, can't you talk to Dad? If you can't talk, can't you write him a letter? Can't I come back to live here again?"

He turned his face to the wall in frustration, and she silently reached out her hand and turned him back to face her.

"I can't? I can't come back? Why not?"

He turned to face the wall again. "Turn off the light, please. How can I sleep when it's so bright?"

She stood up and switched off the light.

The glow from the street lights shone in through the ground-floor window, so she was soon able to make out the clear form of her child in the darkness. There was a deep furrow in the center of his forehead. She laid her hand there and smoothed it out. He frowned again. He lay there with his eyes tightly shut, and even his breathing was muted.

In the late-night darkness that day in June, the smell of waterlogged grass and tree sap mingled with the smells of food waste. After dropping off her son, she walked the nearly two-hour route through the center of Seoul instead of taking the bus. Some of the roads were as brightly lit as they would be in the middle of the day, with suffocating exhaust fumes and blaring music, while others were dark, and decaying, and stray cats tore at rubbish bags with their teeth, and glared at her.

Her legs didn't hurt. She wasn't tired. Illuminated by the pale light in front of the lift, she stood and stared at her front door, the door through which she was now supposed to enter, leading to the bed where she was now supposed to sleep. She turned around and went back out of the building, out into that summer-night smell, the smell of things that had once been alive going bad. She walked faster and faster, until finally she was almost running, throwing herself into the public phone booth in front of the caretaker's lodge, where she pulled all the coins she could find out of her trouser pocket.

She heard a voice. "Hello?"

She opened her mouth. She forced out a breath. She breathed in, and then out again.

The same voice spoke again. "Hello?"

Her hand trembled as it clutched the receiver.

How could you dream of taking him? That far away? And for so long? You bastard. You heartless bastard.

Her teeth chattered and trembled until her spasming fingers put down the phone. She ran her hand roughly over her cheek, almost as if she were slapping her own face. She rubbed away at her philtrum, her jaw, her lips that no one had gagged.

•

That night, for the first time since she lost speech, she looked at herself properly in the mirror. She thought that she must be seeing incorrectly, though she didn't put the thought into words. Surely her eyes couldn't be this serene. She would have been less shocked to see blood or pus or grey sludge running from them. She saw her mute self reflected in her eyes, and in that reflected self saw yet another reflection of her mute self, and another . . . in an endless silence.

The hatred that had boiled up in her a long time ago went on seething, and the agony that used to surge in her remained swollen, a blister that wouldn't burst.

Nothing healed.

Nothing ended.

.

The middle-aged man and the philosophy student, who had been chatting together, must have gone out into the corridor at some point, and now returned, each holding a can of coffee. The man is talking to someone on his mobile, continuing the conversation as he resumes his seat.

"Well, obviously they should have had all staff, rather than the most competent, in mind. What's the point of staff training if only some are following? What's that now, supplementary classes? We're a small business, not a corporation. Have the instructor give me a call tomorrow."

The young philosophy student signals to the man with his eyes and sits back down. He stretches, giving out a low groan as he crunches his neck forward, backward, and side to side. The ten minutes' break time is already up, but today the Greek lecturer, usually so punctual, is late getting back. Suddenly everything becomes quiet.

She is sitting at her desk, motionless as ever. Her back, neck and shoulders are stiff from spending so long in the same position. She opens the notebook and scans the sentences she wrote down during the hour before the break. She jots down words in the blank spaces between the sentences. She perseveres through verb declensions and complicated usages of tense and voice to form simple, incomplete sentences, and waits for her lips and tongue to stir into motion. Waits for the first sound to spring from them.

γῆ κεῖται γυνή.
A woman lies on the ground.

χιὼν ἐπὶ τῇ δειρῇ.
Snow in throat.

ῥύπος ἐπὶ τῷ βλεφάρῳ.
Earth in eyes.

"What's that?" asks the philosophy student, who sits in the same row as her. He points to the notebook, where she's written incomplete sentences in Ancient Greek following on from γῆ γῆ κεῖται γυνή, "A woman lies on the ground," which was one of the examples they'd learned earlier in the lesson. She doesn't get flustered, doesn't hastily shut the notebook. She musters all her strength and looks at the young man's eyes as though into the depths of ice.

The new agony, caused by what her son had told her, could make no crack in her silence; all it did was to leave trails of blood over the frozen surface each day. She spent too long brushing her teeth, too long standing in front of the open refrigerator, banged her leg against the front bumper of a stationary car, or clumsily knocked against a shelf in a shop and sent its goods crashing to the floor. Every time she slipped under the chilly bed sheet and closed her eyes, the snowy street, the unfamiliar pedestrians, the child wearing unfamiliar clothes, the pale face that could have been either her own or that of her son, were waiting for her.

She knew that the passage that led to speech had descended to a still-deeper place, and that if things continued like this she would lose her son for good. The more aware of this she became, the further down that passage buried itself. As though there was some god who, the more earnestly she asked for something, did the reverse of what she asked. She didn't moan, as even that failed to reach her lips, and so she only grew quieter still. Neither blood nor pus flowed from her eyes.

·

"Is it poetry? Poetry written in Greek?" The postgrad student sitting by the window turns to look at her, curiosity etched on his face. Just then, the lecturer comes back into the classroom.

"Seonsaengnim!" The philosophy student chuckles mischievously. "Look, she's been writing poetry in Greek."

In his seat behind the pillar, the middle-aged man turns to look at her, his expression one of amazed admiration, and bursts into loud laughter. Startled by the sound, she closes the notebook. She watches blankly as the lecturer approaches her chair.

"Really? Would you mind if I take a quick look?"

She has to strain herself to concentrate on his words, as if she's deciphering a foreign language. She looks up at his glasses, their pale green lenses so thick they make her eyes swim. All at once she understands the situation, and packs the thick study book, her notebook, dictionary and pencil case in her bag.

"No, please stay seated. You don't have to show it to me."

She stands up, shoulders her bag, pushes her way past the row of empty chairs and heads for the door.

·

In front of the emergency exit that leads to the stairs, someone grabs hold of her arm from behind. Startled, she whips round. It's the first time she's seen the lecturer from this close up. He's shorter than she thought, now that he isn't standing on the raised platform at the front of the classroom, and, oddly, his face suddenly looks aged.

"I didn't mean to make you uncomfortable." Taking a deep breath, he steps closer. "Are you . . . do you maybe not hear what I'm saying?" He raises his hands and makes a gesture. He repeats the same gesture a couple of times, and, as if interpreting himself, haltingly speaks the words, "I'm sorry. I came out to say I'm sorry."

She stares mutely at his face, looks at him as he takes another breath and, undeterred and emphatic, continues signing: "We don't have to talk. You don't have to make any kind of answer. I'm really sorry. I came out to say I'm sorry."

•

The single-lane one-way street runs for a fair stretch alongside the motorway noise barrier. She is walking along its pavement. Not many people go this way, so the council has let it get somewhat neglected. Clumps of grass rise tenaciously from the cracks in the paving slabs. The thick black branches of the acacias, which had been planted in a broad line around the flats in place of a wall, stretch toward one another like arms. The repulsive fug of exhaust fumes mingles with the scent of grass in the humid night air. This close to the road, the roar of car engines slices into her eardrums as sharp skates cut into ice. In the grass at her feet, a grasshopper cries slowly.

It's strange.

It's as if she's already experienced a night exactly like this.

It feels like she's walked this road before, wrapped up in a similar sense of shame and embarrassment.

She would have still had language then, so the emotions would have been clearer, stronger.

But now there are no words inside her.

Words and sentences track her like ghosts, at a remove from her body, but near enough to be within ear- and eyeshot.

It is thanks to that distance that any emotion not strong enough drops away from her like a scrap of weakly adhering tape.

She only looks. She looks, and doesn't translate any of the things that she sees into language.

Images of objects form in her eyes, and they move, fluctuate, or are erased in time with her steps, without ever being translated into words.

·

On one such summer night, a long time ago, she had suddenly started to laugh to herself while walking down a street.

She had looked at the gibbous thirteenth-day moon, and laughed.

Thinking that it resembled someone's sullen face, that its round sunken craters were like eyes concealing disappointment, she had laughed.

As though the words inside her body had first burst out into laughter, and it was that laughter that had spread across her face.

That night when the heat that arrived just past the summer solstice had, as now, withdrawn hesitantly behind the darkness,

that night long ago that was not so long ago,

her child walking ahead of her, while she followed along, cradling a huge cold watermelon in her arms.

Her voice had been affectionate as it gently diffused outwards, trying to take up the minimum of space.

Her lips hadn't shown signs of gritted teeth.

Blood had not gathered in her eyes.

8

χαλεπὰ τὰ καλά

Chalepa ta kala.

The beautiful is beautiful.
The beautiful is noble.
The beautiful is difficult.

It was possible for all three translations to be correct, because beauty, difficulty and nobleness were, for the Ancient Greeks, concepts not yet split apart. As 빛, bhit, in my mother tongue has always meant both "brightness" and "hue," a light that is both clarity and color.

It was the first Buddha's Birthday since I had left Germany and returned to Seoul. I sought out the temple in Suyuri, where I'd gone with my mother and younger sister all those years ago, though now

I was alone. Back when we still lived here, the road that led up to the temple had been flanked on both sides by potato fields; today, those fields were smothered by cement, and residential low-rises had been built over them. Only once I'd passed beneath the temple's iljumun, its first gate, was I able to see how the temple itself had escaped the passage of time. There were no new extensions, and the pagoda and bell pavilion seemed, if anything, to have shrunk. But of course I was the one who had grown.

Back then, I was still able to move about freely at night, and so I wandered aimlessly around the temple grounds while I waited for it to grow dark. There were fewer hanji lanterns than I remembered; perhaps the number of devotees had dwindled, with the elderly having passed away. The beauty alone was unchanged. In fact, I found it even more beautiful than I had when I lacked an adult's deep and measured attention. If the lantern festival of my childhood had been a spectacle of pure wonderment, there was something in it this time that cut through to my core.

Eventually, once it was fully dark, I sat on the maru of the public hall and watched the light ripple up the insides of the red-and-white lanterns at each gust of wind. That there had once been a word that encapsulated both beauty and the sacred, without their having yet fallen away from each other, just as color and clarity had formed one body within another word—the truth of this had never before been brought home to me with such vibrant intensity. Only when it was close to eleven o'clock, when the door to the main hall closes, did I stir myself to get up.

I headed toward the entrance gate, muttering, "Time to go home." It would take thirty minutes to reach the main road where the bus stop was, then another hour on the bus to get home—

suddenly I was gripped by the thought that the bus might never arrive at my door. A strange sense that, no matter how many times I changed between bus and subway, I would never find the way back, never break outside of that vivid night.

The feeling was not unfamiliar. It was embedded in the ceaselessly recurring dreams I'd had since my teens, when I began my new life in Germany. In these dreams it was always dusk, I was on a bus, and the shopfront signs in the street outside bore unfamiliar writing that was neither my mother tongue nor German. My dream-self always wanted to alight from this wrong bus I'd taken, but didn't know which bus was the right one, or how to get to another bus stop. Nor could I recall my original destination. There was nothing I could do but stay where I was, sitting at the back, staring out into the streets that were darkening moment by moment.

Suppressing the indescribable emotion that dream stirred up in me even now, an emotion frightening in its very recurrence, I carried on putting one foot in front of the other. The night air was cold. The red hanji lanterns strung up in layered rows overhead were shaking soundlessly, shrouded as ever in perfect beauty and serenity.

"The world is an illusion, and living is dreaming," I muttered.

Yet blood runs and tears gush forth.

9

Dusk

Have you tried walking in the morning half-light?

The morning hours when you move through the cold air, one foot in front of the other, with a real sense of just how warm and tender the human body is. The morning hours when a blue-tinged light seeps from the bodies of all material things, penetrating your newly sleep-shorn eyes, miraculous.

Back when we lived in the first-floor apartment at the end of Kriegkstrasse, the early hours of the dawn inevitably found me walking the alleys alone like that. When I came back home, around the time that the blue tinge dissipated from the air, you and our parents would still be asleep. Feeling the urge to brighten the interior of the house, which was darker than the streets outside, I would flick on the shaded lamp, and a clean hunger would lead me to the fridge. I would pick out a handful of walnuts, tossing them into my mouth one by one as I tiptoed to my room.

Now all such things have become impossible for me—since I am able to move around as I please solely at those times of day that are bright enough, in places that are bright enough. I can only imagine it: leaving the house I now rent at around sunrise, passing through the darkened streets emptied of vehicles and pedestrians; my body, walking on and on until I arrive at the house in Suyuri where we lived all those years ago.

You remember our house in Suyuri?

A four-room flat in a low-rise, fairly spacious for those times but difficult to heat in the winters, the drafts were so severe. Mother would complain that the eastward-facing aspect made it too cold, but I preferred it. Wandering into the living room at dawn, I felt as though all the furniture was wrapped in a blue cloth. A scene was playing out in which blue threads were being ceaselessly spun out, filling the chilly air in front of me, and I would stand there in my long johns and stare at it, entranced. At the time, I had no idea that what seemed such a captivating hallucination was caused by my weakening eyesight.

You remember our little chick, which we called Ppibi?

You weren't old enough to go to school when I came home with that warm bundle, a chick the vendor at the school gate had slipped into a paper bag, and watched you turn bright red with pleasure. Getting mother's permission to keep it was purely down to your incessant pestering.

But barely two months later we were breaking a pair of wooden chopsticks and binding them with cotton to make a cross. We hadn't yet seen the gravestone and offering stone at our family's burial plot, so we imitated the illustrations in Western children's books.

The earth in the building's shared flowerbed was frozen hard. Your eyes swollen from having cried all night, you stopped trying to gouge the frozen earth out with a spoon, saying your hands were freezing. My own spoon was already severely bent, defeated by the solid ground, while Ppibi lay quiet as ever, wrapped in a white gauze towel.

I actually went in search of that place, the first winter I came back here.

The low-rise had been pulled down. In its place stood a new commercial building that was two stories higher. Where the flower-beds had been were white lines demarcating parking bays, and two cars, a van and a mini-truck, were parked side by side. Looking at those cars, whose windscreens and side mirrors were completely frosted over, gazing at the white steam escaping from my mouth, I wondered absentmindedly: what became of them, those small bones?

Dearest Ran,

I got the letter and CD you sent.

I wrote a reply the very same night I received them; I wasn't happy with how it came out, so this is my second go. For some reason, whenever I write something these days, it comes out lifeless and banal.

In any case, quite the opposite of what you were worrying about in your letter is true: I'm doing fine.

I'm getting regular treatment from a trustworthy doctor, and I cook for myself and eat at the proper times. In the mornings I do some light exercises for half an hour, and later in the day I go on fairly long walks through the alleys.

In fact, if there's anyone whose health is a matter for concern, it's you. Aren't you someone who lives with fire in your chest? Don't you neglect yourself whenever you're focused on something, push yourself so hard that you reach the point of making yourself ill?

"The brother might as well be a girl and the little sister a boy." That's how our relatives described us, pitting us against each other. You hated hearing those words, hated being told to arrange your drawers neatly, like I did. To pack your satchel the night before, like I did. To write in a neat hand, like I did. To be polite and look adults in the face, like I did. You used to bawl out Mum with your foghorn voice: "Can't you give it a rest?" "I'm so worked up I'm boiling." "I'd jump in the fridge if that would help."

Do you still feel like that, Ran?

Do you get so angry you want to jump in the fridge?

Are you using rehearsals as an excuse to eat muesli twice a day and call it a meal, like you did when you were a student?

Have things improved with the ensemble leader, the one you don't get along with?

Have you phoned Mother recently?

How are her knees?

Does she seem like she's doing okay, on her own?

My work at the academy, which you and Mother combine your strengths to worry about, is going smoothly as always. Mother is forever fretting that I will end up penniless, but that my pride means I won't breathe a word of it to anyone. Will you please let her know that they recently added another beginner's Latin course, which means I now teach four classes a week? As we have only a few students, it's not at all taxing to teach more classes, and I enjoy the lessons, as the students are all of mature age, and cultured. You can also tell her that for the first two or three years after I came back here, I occasionally sought out East Asian classics to read, and became quite friendly with a few students while asking them about the parts I didn't understand—now I think of it, it's been a while since I got in touch with them. To be honest, there are times when I feel envious watching the students. Of their certainty, their unwavering firmness, perhaps—something only those whose life, language and culture have never been broken in two, as they have for us, are able to possess.

Dearest Ran,

There is, in fact, one particular student who's caught my interest, whom I'm quite attentive to these days.

With only a small number of students, I'm able to sense what piques their interest by the look on their face or by their body language; this person was never interested in any of the texts we covered. Not in Greek philosophy, in works of literature, or in the New Testament passages that are sometimes quoted. Yet it wasn't laziness; on the contrary, she never had a single absence from class. I feel that she pays attention only to the interesting elements of language itself—the grammar and the turns of phrase.

But what's more peculiar is that this person never says anything, never even laughs. When I call the register at the beginning of class, she doesn't answer, and she doesn't chat with anyone during the break. At first I thought she was just shy; but when I realized that an entire six months had gone by without her ever having opened her mouth, I had to wonder.

One time, when I went back into the classroom as the break ended, one of the students laughingly told me that the woman had written poetry in Greek. Curious, I told her I'd like to take a look. The woman fixed me with a stare, then got up from her seat and left the classroom.

It was then that it suddenly occurred to me: this might be someone who can neither hear nor speak. Who'd been just about following my classes by reading my lips all this time. And who had therefore been unable to respond, whether to jokes or to questions.

I hastily ran out into the corridor. I grabbed hold of her arm as she was making her way down the dark emergency stairs, as I knew I wouldn't be able to see her without the bright overhead lighting. I told her I was sorry, in speech and in sign. I asked if she was unable to hear. Said that I hadn't known. That it had absolutely not been my intention to make her uncomfortable. I realized soon enough that I was signing in German Sign Language, but, not knowing Korean Sign Language, I couldn't think of what else to do.

Making no response whatsoever, she stared fixedly across at me. I wonder if I can explain to you the strange despair I felt just then. There was something frightening in that woman's silence, something terrible. Long ago, when I lifted up dead Ppibi's body to wrap it in the white gauze . . . like the deathly hush I felt when I peeked into the small hollow that we'd gouged in the frozen ground with our spoons.

Can you imagine it?

I'd never seen such silence in someone who was alive.

Dearest Ran,

I received the letter and CD you sent the other day.

My reply's a little late, I know.

I don't write so well these days.

It's no great cause for concern.

I don't spend so much time reading books, you see. Just as Mother always hoped would happen.

Spending more of my free time sitting quietly or strolling through the bright streets, perhaps it's become that much more awkward to pick up a pen and put the finishing touches to whatever short piece of writing is on my desk.

Instead, I'm listening to your CD almost every day.

Listening carefully to pick out the soprano part within the harmony, I think to myself in surprise at times: that's your voice.

There it must be dusk.

Still the surroundings must be bright, with one or two lights on in the shops. Pedestrians will be bustling back and forth through the streets. At the tram stop, evening commuters will be milling around, while those wanting to catch the underground will be hurrying down the stairs, past the homeless people.

Here it is now deep night.

I'm listening to your CD with the window open and the volume down, humming along now and then, as I write this letter.

Do you remember the summer nights here?

The air, refreshingly damp as though compensating for the sticky heat of the daylight hours.

The deep spill of darkness.

The alleyways where the scent of grass, of the sap from the broadleaf trees, spreads thickly.

The noise of car engines, which can be heard until the dead of night.

The insects crying all night long in the dark forest of weeds leading up the nearby mountain.

Your song is flowing out into the heart of it.

Perhaps I can admit this now.

I used to complain that it was too loud when you practiced, and you were so hot-blooded that you used to argue me into a corner with the volume of your well-trained voice, but this you probably wouldn't have been able to guess: that the first winter I spent in Germany, finding Frankfurt even colder than Seoul, and exhausted by an unfamiliar classroom, language and people, I would return home to sit in the corridor outside our flat, with my back against the wall, and listen to your singing seeping out from the front door. How your voice caressed my face.

The following winter, after we'd moved to Mainz for its cheap rent, when you were on the cusp of adolescence, you said something once that's stayed with me. Mother was out late, working at the grocery store she'd opened that catered to Asian people, and we were sitting together at the bare dining table eating horribly bland muesli, when you mumbled, head bowed, that there were times when the silence that gaped between the poor instrument that was your body and the song you were about to sing felt as terrifying as a precipice.

Then you stared at me with the face of the six-year-old girl who had told me your hands were freezing, and gave me a look that seemed to say nothing made sense anymore. And I realized that your voice wasn't capable of caressing your face the way it did mine. Then what possibly could, I wondered. I suppose I was despairing.

Did you ever despair of me?

Having heard from Mother that I had bought a plane ticket to Incheon, you took the night train to see me the day before you had a final rehearsal. With your coat collar folded inwards on one side and an elegant scarf, white, pale green and pale yellow, wound around and around your neck to stop your vocal cords from getting damaged in the cold air. "I don't understand you, oppa," you said. "I thought you loved us."

What a strange thing one's flesh and blood is.

How strange are the ways that it brings us sorrow.

When we were so soft and easily broken, when we moved from one side of the world to the other, we were like two eggs in one basket, like two ceramic balls that had been formed from the same earthen dough. It was in the company of your scowling, crying, laughing face that my childhood cracked, broke, was put back together unharmed, and so passed.

Sometimes I'll burst out laughing from remembering the games we used to play. How we would invent nicknames and tease each other. How I used to carry you on my back, and we'd exchange words in singsong: "How far along are we, / We're as far as the bus stop. / How far along are we, / We're as far as far can be." That brief period when I was stronger than you and able to look after you.

The sight of you endlessly cutting up colored paper to glue on to the house we'd made for Ppibi out of a corrugated-cardboard box.

Ppibi, who died crying ppi-i-ppi-i from early evening until the dead of night, and you all wrung out from crying as you watched over him; how Father in his pajamas glared at Ppibi, then at you, and yelled, "Get that thing out of here!"

Crying your heart out, you pummeled his stomach with your small fists. You sank your teeth into his thighs.

Dearest Ran,

Do you sometimes think of Father?

Since he loved you—since he often took you to places like the zoo or the amusement park or to cafés, holding your hand—do you have memories of him that I don't?

He didn't like me. As numerous strangers had done throughout our childhood, he compared us with each other. He would tell Mother I was as meek as a girl, a dull boy who knew nothing but study, when what he needed was a son who was as outgoing and frank as Ran, a son who would grow up into a real man. But I knew that what he really disliked wasn't my temperament but my eyes. He never looked me in the eyes. If our gaze did happen to meet, he would slowly, calmly, look away. He was a heartless man. He'd climbed the ladder of his organization in no time to become an executive at a young age. Had tendered his resignation only a year after being appointed as the person in charge of the German branch. Had disappeared one day, without saying a word to anyone about where he was going. When he showed up out of the blue six months later, he had to have an immediate eye operation, and after the operation was unsuccessful and we moved as a family to Mainz, he made no attempt to stir out of the flat's innermost room, even to his last breath.

Did he ever tell you?

Where he hid himself away for those six months?

Within which city's twilight he'd waited, like me, before returning?

I want to ask him, without the least pity or even a trace of affection, what he looked at and listened to during that brief time.

And whether this twilight does, in fact, lead to total night.

Had I asked him these things when he was still alive, would that heartless person have sneered at me? Without the glasses that he had come not to need anymore, would he have stared wordlessly in my direction with those empty eyes that yawned beneath his shapely brows?

Dearest, much-missed Ran,

Pig-headed, foghorn-voiced Ran.

You know that I am someone who is unable to obtain wisdom from suffering, don't you? That my inner eyes will never open, even as my sight dulls. That I am bound to lose my way amid my countless chaotic memories, my acute emotions. That I wait in my innate foolishness. Not even knowing what I wait for, but tenacious all the same.

Now your CD has played all the way through,
  the night has grown deeper than it was not long before.
  Your voice soaks into the quiet,
  until this quiet somehow comes to feel warm.

I'll have to wait another three hours for the sun to come up.
  I'll have to let myself doze off before then, if only for a moment.
  Now when I switch off the desk light, the darkness will come crowding in.
  The night of my eyes, deeper than ink, in which there is almost no difference between their being closed or open.

But would you believe me if I told you that every night I switch off the lights without despairing? Knowing I'll open them anew at daybreak. Knowing I'll open the window and look out at the dark sky beyond the mosquito screen. Knowing I will throw on a light jumper and walk outside, if only in my imagination. That I will make my way one step at a time over the dark pavements. I will see the fabric of darkness, unraveled into bluish threads, wind about the city—a true spectacle. I'll polish my glasses and put them on, open both eyes as wide as possible and dip my face in that brief blue light. Do you believe it? My heart is fluttering at the mere thought of it.

10

παθεῖν
μαθεῖν

"These two verbs mean 'to suffer' and 'to learn.' Do you see how they're almost identical? What Socrates is doing here is punning on these words to remark on the similarity of the two actions."

She extracts the hexagonal pencil that she had been absentmindedly leaning on with her elbow. After rubbing her smarting skin, she copies the two words written on the blackboard into her notebook. She writes them first using the Greek alphabet, then tries but ultimately fails to write the meaning next to them in her own language. Instead, she raises her left fist and rubs her sleepless eyes. She looks up at the pallid face of the Greek lecturer. At the chalk clutched in his hand, the letters of her mother tongue like withered bloodstains, but white, distinct on the blackboard.

"However, we cannot see the twinning of these verbs simply as a play on words. Since, for Socrates, learning literally meant suffering. Even granting that Socrates himself did not think this in so many words, the thought was at least formulated as such by the young Plato."

The middle-aged man sitting next to the pillar slurps his vending-machine coffee, which must be cold now. Since last week, at the man's suggestion, their classes have been pushed back to eight o'clock—as he was having to skip dinner to make it on time from work—but, if anything, he looks even more drowsy and fatigued than before, perhaps because of the food in his stomach. The philosophy student has been absent since last week, likely having gone back to his hometown now that the term has ended, and the postgrad is twitching his lips to pronounce soundlessly the Greek words, his face tense as always. He told the philosophy student that he was hoping, after he finished his master's degree in the history of medicine, to be selected for a scholarship that would enable him to study Greek medicine in the UK; it was being sponsored by a pharmaceutical company, which would provide his living expenses as well as his tuition for the duration. Occasionally he turned up carrying a copy of Galen in the original, of which every single page was full of underlining; and the Greek lecturer would be flustered by his requests for interpretations of the anatomy sections. When the postgrad complained of the difficulty of interpreting the original text, the lecturer told him, his face creased with mirth, "Europeans find Ancient Greek just as difficult. Just as difficult as young Kore-

ans find reading and understanding texts in Classical Chinese . . .
So don't aim for anything too perfect."

". . . after the oracle at the shrine of Delphi pronounced him the
wisest man in Athens, the latter part of his life began, which could
not be called anything but a chaotic mess. He took up a spot at the
entrance to the market, like a beggar, a quarreler, a lay priest, to
stand there and repeatedly say that he knew nothing. He didn't
know a single thing; please would someone, anyone at all, teach
him wisdom? The rest of his life was spent in learning without a
teacher, and in the terrible ordeal whose conclusion everyone is
now well aware of."

As ever, she is looking up at the Greek lecturer's wan face. The
words of her mother tongue that are scribbled on the blackboard
have been soundlessly kneaded into the inside of her right fist, into
the slick surface of the sweat-damp pencil. She knows those words,
but also doesn't know them. Nausea is waiting for her. She is able to
relate to those words, and yet she is not. She is able to write them,
and yet she is not. She bows her head. Exhales carefully. *Doesn't
wish to breathe in.* Breathes in deeply.

11

Night

The flat she rents is dark.

It's on the ground floor of the apartment complex; the darkness is because the living room faces a dense wooded area. She'd rented it because she liked having a view of the tall trees' lower trunks; she hadn't considered that the woods would leave the living room in shadow even in the daytime.

Back when her son still lived with her, they'd kept the triphosphor fluorescent lamps on all day, as these were said to be closer to sunlight, but now she cannot feel the need. She spends the majority of her time in the darkened living room, where it is impossible to gauge the weather outside. She almost never goes into the bedroom, with its double bed, wardrobe and television that she used to share with her son. It's the same with the small room with the raw timber desk and bookcase she'd had custom-made for him. That room is the sole bright spot in her house, where the trees' shadows do not fall, but the door stays closed except on the days when the child is visiting.

Directly after her mother's funeral—when she and her son were still together, when she was still speaking—she pulled out clothes to wear for her year of mourning and hung them on a sixty-centimeter-wide clothes rack. A black cotton spring-and-autumn shirt and a black short-sleeved blouse. One pair of black cotton trousers and one pair of black jeans. A black turtleneck sweater and a long black woolen coat. A thickly knitted black muffler and a pair of dark grey gloves.

"There. I won't have to buy anything else," she muttered to herself, standing in front of the rack, and her son, who had been perched on the bed watching what she was doing, asked, "Why do you have to wear only black for a whole year?"

She replied calmly, "So as not to be cheerful, I guess."

"Are you not allowed to be cheerful?"

"I'd feel bad."

"For Grandma? But Grandma would want you to be happy, Mum!"

Only then did she look back at her son and smile.

·

Her lifestyle is simple.

She launders her few black outfits without delay, shops for the minimum of groceries at the nearby store, prepares the minimum of food and, after eating, promptly tidies everything away. In the daytime hours when she is not occupied with those basic tasks, she generally sits unmoving on the living-room sofa looking out at the tall trees' verdant branches and thick lower trunks. The house grows dark when it is still not yet evening. Around the time when the trees' contours grow black, she opens the front door and goes out. She passes through the apartment complex as dusk is falling, reaches the pedestrian crossing where the green light doesn't stay on for long and carries on walking.

She walks in order to exhaust herself to the point of no longer being able to walk. She walks until she is unable to register the quiet of the house to which she must now return, until she has no strength left to cast her gaze over the black woods, the black curtains, the black sofa, the black Lego boxes. She walks until, giddy with tiredness, she will be able to lie down on her side on the sofa and fall asleep without washing or tugging a quilt over herself. She walks so that she will not wake in the middle of the night even if plagued by nightmares, so that she will not toss and turn with her eyes open until dawn, unable to achieve sleep again. She walks so that, in those vivid dawn hours, she will not have to doggedly recall and piece together the broken shards of memories.

On Thursdays, when there is a Greek class, she packs her bag a little earlier than she needs to. After alighting from the bus several stops before the academy, she walks, enduring the afternoon heat radiating from the tarmac. Even after she slips into the building's shadowed interior, her whole body is drenched in sweat for a while.

Once, she had just gone up to the first floor when she saw the Greek lecturer walking ahead of her. She stopped in her tracks instinctively. She held her breath so as not to make a sound. Having already sensed someone's presence, he turned to look back over his shoulder and smiled. It was a smile that mingled closeness, awkwardness and resignation, and made it clear that he had been about to greet her, then brought himself up short. Now it faded into an earnest expression, as if he were formally asking her to excuse his initial familiarity.

After that day, when she happened to bump into him on the stairs or in the corridor, he did not smile but greeted her faintly with his eyes. Up until the moment they entered the empty classroom, one through the rear door and one through the front, they walked with a similar stride. With their upper bodies leaning forward at a similar angle and their bags slung over their shoulders. Calmly aware of each other's presence.

.

There is a particular expression his face assumes when he addresses someone. His gaze humbly requests the other person's consent; there are occasionally times when something other than deference, something like an inexplicable, delicate sadness, haunts his look.

It was around thirty minutes before the lesson's start, and they were the only ones in the classroom. After taking her seat, she got out her textbook and writing things from her bag one by one, distractedly raised her head, and their eyes met. He stood up from his own chair, which was placed next to the lectern, and approached a desk that was at a little distance from hers. After pulling out the chair and making space, he sat down facing the aisle. He raised both hands and lightly interlaced them in the air; it was just for a few moments, but she thought he was asking for a handshake. He was quiet for a while with his hands interlaced like that. As though he were making up his mind whether or not to address her and would let her know in due course. Not long afterward there was the sound of footsteps in the corridor, and he stood up and went back to his place next to the lectern.

.

There are times when they look at each other without speaking. Waiting for the lesson to begin. After the lesson has begun. In the corridor during breaks, in front of the office. Little by little, his face became familiar to her. His once-unremarkable features, expressions, frame and postures became distinctive. But she did not assign any meaning to this, having never thought about the change in words.

.

It is a sweltering July night.

The two fans set up on either side of the blackboard are rotating with fierce intensity. The windows on either side of the classroom are flung wide open.

"This world is ephemeral and beautiful, is it not," he says.

"But rather than this ephemeral and beautiful world, Plato wanted one that was eternal and beautiful."

The postgrad, who had been almost over-earnest in every lesson so far, has been nodding off for the last twenty minutes. The man behind the pillar, after repeatedly wiping the nape of his neck with a handkerchief, has fallen asleep with his forehead on his desk, as though finally succumbing to exhaustion. Only she and the philosophy student are awake. When the breeze from the oscillating fan pulls away from him, the youth instantly starts fluttering a long fan made of hanji to cool his sweat.

"The *Republic* is actually a dynamic text. It draws the reader in through the energetic progression of its reasoning alone. Now and then in the development of an argument, at the narrow and dangerous passages . . . well, to speak metaphorically, every time he steps to the edge of the cliff, Plato borrows Socrates's voice to ask the reader, 'Are you following me?' As a reckless leader of a climbing party looks back over his shoulder to check on the others. He knows that this is a dangerous soliloquy, that he is, in fact, answering his own question, as do we who are reading."

With his placid gaze behind the pale green lenses, he looks directly at her clear eyes. Perhaps because the students are especially unfocused today, for close on ten minutes he has been explaining the content of the text rather than its grammar. At some point, the nature of these reading classes has come loosely to straddle Greek language and philosophy.

"People who, though they believe in beautiful objects, do not believe in beauty itself, Plato deemed such people to be in a state of dreaming, and was convinced that one could be persuaded that this was the case through reasoning. In his world, everything was upside down like this. That is to say, he considered that he himself was awake and not dreaming. He who, rather than trusting in the beautiful objects of reality, trusted only in an absolute beauty that cannot exist in reality."

·

Passing in front of the office with her bag slung over her shoulder after the class was over, she sees him talking to the part-time admin with bobbed hair. The young woman is engrossed in explaining the features of her new smartphone. Bending forward at the waist, he has his face practically pressed up against the phone and it appears as though his glasses are about to collide with it. The posture makes him look more diminutive than he is. The woman speaks rapidly in a high-pitched voice.

"See, this is a real-time webcam broadcast from a colony of penguins at the South Pole. It cools me down when the heat's unbearable. Hmm, looks like it's night there too. Here, do you see them? The penguins are already all asleep . . . What, this? The dark purplish bit? I told you, that's the sea. The whitish bit is ice. It's all glaciers. Wow, it's just started snowing. See? The shining specks here . . . can't you see?"

·

Slipping out of the main door of the faded academy building, she sees the postgrad standing by the dark wall, on the phone to someone. An unlit cigarette held between his fingers, he speaks in a low whisper, not realizing that she is passing by, and says, through clenched teeth: "I told you I won't ask you for help, just don't stand in my way. It's the money I need to study abroad. The money I've worked my fingers to the bone to save up, the reason I don't yet have a master's at my age. You'll be ruined whether or not I give you every won of it, won't you, Father? Ruined, and ruined again, and again, forever."

·

When the Greek lesson is over, she walks the dark streets as she has always done. The vehicles on the road speed past daringly as they always do. Motorbikes carrying midnight snacks in red metal boxes weave in and out of the traffic, ignoring both lanes and lights. Past drunks young or old, weary workers in skirt suits or short-sleeved shirts, elderly women staring blankly from the entrances of empty restaurants, she carries on walking.

She arrives at the bustling intersection of an eight-lane and a four-lane road. Buildings soar up in the distance, enormous digital billboards blazing from their tops. As always, she stops in front of the pedestrian crossing and looks up at those screens. Faces larger than life move enormous lips to speak inaudible words. Giant letters flow along the bottoms of the screens, twitching their mouths like fish. Giant, magnified news screens flash past: corpses on stretchers, crowds, a flaming airplane, wailing women.

Before she knows it, the light goes green. Crossing the black tarmac from which the radiant heat has not yet cooled, she walks toward the street opposite. The LED signs go on mutely emitting their stream of giant images and letters. A sleek car racing silently across a vast desert, an actress in a low-cut dress laughing sound-lessly, flicker like ghosts above the black street.

·

By the time she arrives at the huge river that cuts across the city, her dusty face is gleaming with sweat. She continues along the walkway of the riverside path, which seems to stretch on forever. The lights reflected in the dark river bob up and down. She has knots in her calves, and the soles of her feet in her thin sandals feel on fire. The humid black wind rising off the surface of the water slowly cools her body.

She cannot know that, afloat in the air she has breathed in every night since last spring, were infinitesimal luminous bodies, which have inadvertently entered her respiratory system and are still twinkling there. She cannot know the elements that, faintly brightening the interstices of her cells, are transparently passing through and drifting within. Xenon and cesium-137. Radioactive iodine-131, which has a short half-life and will soon disappear. She is ignorant of the particles of stodgy red blood that are flowing unrelentingly through her veins. She is ignorant of her black lungs and muscles and viscera, of the hot heart powerfully pumping.

·

She enters the underpass and carries on walking. She walks past shops with their shutters already down, past those where the lights are just being switched off. She passes a pair of near-senseless drunks, engaged in a hopeless fight outside a public toilet. After reaching the end of the underpass, elongated like an alimentary canal, she is disgorged on to the dark streets. She makes her way over a dangerous crossing whose traffic lights aren't working, where an orange signal light is blinking. She passes along a road that is like a ruin, with no one about, where dozens of cars huddle soundlessly in a black public car park. She passes through the bleak downtown area again. She passes noisy down-at-heel bars. She passes drunks walking out into the middle of the road, risking their necks to hail a taxi. She passes lewd looks that shamelessly meet her gaze, and the unfocused pupils of indifferent eyes.

When midnight is near, she discovers that she has arrived at the entrance to an unfamiliar cinema. The lights are off in the booth; all the tickets for the final film have been sold. Without realizing what she is doing she approaches the booth's translucent acrylic partition. She brings her lips close to its eight black holes, then flinches away. As if a terrifying force might blast out of those neat, orderly holes and forcibly aspirate her voice from her lips and throat.

·

The bus stop in front of the theatre is dark and dirty. She stands among crumpled beer cans, empty fizzy-drink bottles, plastic bags, someone's spit, scattered bits of trampled popcorn. She is done with walking now. She sees a bus approaching that might be the last one of the night. It doesn't go by her house, but it will take her to the area.

The moment she steps up on to the bus, she is startled by the incredibly strong air conditioning. Inside, in the dim light, around a dozen passengers sit in silence. It is a silence thick with fatigue, a sense of defeat, and something like hostility worn faint over time.

She walks down the aisle to where there is an empty double-seat. A late-night drama flows out from the muted television installed behind the driver's seat. A man and a woman are quarreling soundlessly, then they break off and bring their lips together in a fierce, long embrace. The color setting is wrong, and the screen has a blue tinge.

•

She doesn't look at the television screen. Terrible fatigue rushes in on her, and yet, though she shuts her eyes, sleep evades her. She has goosebumps on her arms and the back of her neck from the aggressive air conditioning. She looks out of the window. The bus is cutting through the streets of the city, which is lit up all night. Muffins and slices of cake in various colors are displayed in the clear-glass fridges of dazzlingly illuminated cafés. A fake diamond necklace glitters in the display case of a jewelry shop closed for the night. On an enormous poster covering one side of a building, a familiar male actor is laughing, crinkling the fine wrinkles around his eyes. A woman in a short dress and unseasonal leather boots raises the hand clutching her mobile to hail a taxi. On the stairs in front of a shuttered bunsik bar, a man with grey-streaked hair is lying huddled on some newspaper.

•

She remembers the kaleidoscope she made at primary school. She joined three rectangular pieces of a mirror, which she'd had cut in a mirror shop, to make a triangular prism, then scissored colored paper into tiny pieces and put them inside. She was instantly captivated by the strange world that unfolded inside each time she held one end up to her eye and shook the kaleidoscope.

After losing words, there were times when that world rose up in front of her eyes, overlaying whatever scene was already there. When, exhausted as she was now, a bus bore her through the night streets' solid black forest. When walking up the dark, narrow stairs of the academy building. When passing down the long corridor that led to the classroom. When gazing at afternoon sunlight, quiet and trees, leaves, the patterns of yellow light between them. When walking beneath the neon signs and colored bulbs that flashed noisily, as if fit to burst.

Once she lost words, all such scenery became fragmented, each piece distinct and separate—like the colored paper inside the kaleidoscope, shifting silently, repeatedly and in concert to form new patterns.

．

Her son was six.

For once it was a leisurely Sunday morning, and, after an aimless conversation, she suggested to him that they come up with names for themselves based on what natural thing they most resembled. Her son liked the idea, claimed "Sparkling Forest" for himself, then named her too. Decisively, as though it fitted her exactly.

"Thickly Falling Snow's Sorrow."

"What?"

"That's your name, Mum."

Not knowing what to say, she peered into his clear eyes.

•

The shards of memories shift and form patterns. Without particular context, without overall perspective or meaning. They scatter; suddenly, decisively, they come together. Like innumerable butterflies stilling the movement of their wings as one. Like unfeeling dancers who obscure their faces.

The outer ring road of Gwangju, where she spent her childhood, appears to her in that way.

As does the summer when she was nine. The national holiday afternoon when she crossed the road near the house, walking behind the white dog she had raised for almost five years. A car going faster than the limit struck the dog like a bolt of lightning and screamed away, a hit-and-run. The lower part of the dog's torso was stuck fast to the warm tarmac that had been laid only a few days before, flat as a sheet of paper. With only its front legs, chest and head still in solid, three-dimensional form, the dog groaned, foaming at the mouth. She raced over heedlessly and tried to embrace the dog. The dog, using all its strength, sank its teeth into her shoulder, her chest. She couldn't even scream. She tried to block the dog's mouth with her arms. The moment it bit her wrist for the second time, she fainted, and by the time the grown-ups had come running over the dog was dead.

The flooded rice paddies that gleamed in all directions, in every place her gaze touched, appear in that way.

It was the spring when she was twenty, that long day when the body of her dead father had been transported from the night-duty guard room where he'd worked to their family burial ground on the outskirts of Gwangju. As if the whole world had been turned into a fish tank, the glittering paddy fields stretched out as far as the eye could see, brimming with dazzling, deep blue water.

The strange dream in which her lips swell up blackish-red appears in that way.

In that recurring dream, she sees blood and pus flow from the place where a blister has burst. She watches her front tooth shudder at the root as though eager to shake itself loose, and when she spits out saliva she sees that it comes mixed with a mouthful of blood. She sees a hand, she cannot tell whose, plug her mouth fast with sterile cotton rolls that are as firm as pebbles. Decisively, as though wanting to stopper both blood and screams.

·

After alighting from the bus, she resumes walking.

She walks without rest the distance of five or six bus stops, at one point turning into a one-way street where fragments of concrete that had once formed the pavement lie broken.

Because the bus's air conditioning had been too strong, the sweltering night still feels pleasantly warm.

Pushing aside the grass that has straggled up through each crack in the concrete, she walks.

Between the black leather straps of her sandals, moisture beads her bare skin.

·

Makes no judgments.
Ascribes no emotions.

Everything appears as fragments,
scatters as fragments. Disappears.

Words grow a little more distant from the body.
Emotions that had saturated them,
like heavy layers of shadow,
like stench and nausea,
like something viscous, fall away.
Like tiles that, long under water, have lost their adhesiveness.
Like a part of one's flesh that has rotted without one's knowing.

.

Having had sweat soak it, then dry on it, repeatedly from morning until night, her clammy body is now reflected in the mirror that hangs above the sink. She steps into the bathtub, which is half full of warm water. Curls her dust-covered body into the most comfortable position. She drifts into sleep without realizing it, and only when the water is almost stone cold does she shiver and start awake.

.

She carefully touches her lips to her sleeping child's eyelids. She lies down beside him and closes her eyes. If she opens her eyes, it seems she will see the thickly falling snow, so she closes them even more tightly. With her eyes closed, none of it is visible. Neither the big glittering hexagonal crystals, nor the flakes soft as feathers. Neither the deep purple sea, nor the glacier like a white mountain peak. There are neither words nor color for her until the night is over. Everything is covered by the thick snow. A snow that is like time, time that fractured as it froze, settles ceaselessly over her stiff body. The child by her side isn't there. Lying motionless at the bed's chilly edge, she calls the dream into being, over and over again, to kiss her son's warm eyelids.

12

The postgrad raises his fleshy hand and asks the Greek lecturer a question. His earnest, resonant voice rings out in the quiet class-room. His sweat-soaked grey striped T-shirt clings to his back and armpits, making a pattern of darker grey.

"I'm wondering about the difference between the divine, τὸ δαιμόνιον, to daimonion, and the sacred, τὸ θεῖον, to theion. In the previous class you said that θεώρειν, theoria, also means 'to look'; is the sacred, to theion, also related to the verb 'to look'? And, in that case, are the gods perhaps beings that look, or the look itself?"

Now the philosophy student sitting next to her asks a question. He has a slight Daegu accent. The lock screen of the mobile phone that he has just set down is a photo of him with a short-haired girl in a white T-shirt, the two of them holding up their arms to make a big heart shape.

"In the part that argues everything has within it that which harms it, he uses the example of how the inflammation of the eye ruins the eye and blinds it, and how rust ruins iron and completely shatters it. Why, then, isn't the human soul, which is analogous to such things, ruined by its foolish, bad attributes?"

13

The sun was not yet up.

Someone came into my room, touched my shoulder and handed me a letter. After rubbing my eyes, getting up and thanking them, I ripped open the envelope, which was completely blank, to find a single sheet of snow-white paper, neatly folded twice. Unfolding it, I could tell by the feel of the paper that the letter was written in Braille.

I began cautiously to grope my way through the sentences, line by line, until I had reached the end. I understood nothing. I couldn't even tell whether it was written in Korean Braille or in another Braille alphabet. Only then did it occur to me that I had never learned Braille.

I placed this anonymous, unfathomable letter on my knee; I may have trembled a little. What response should I now give to the messenger? I couldn't recall the face of the person who had handed me the letter and remained standing by my pillow.

I looked up, and, as I did so, I thought I'd woken from a dream about the letter. But I was still dreaming. There was no one in the room. As though one of the mornings of my childhood had come back to me, every object entered my field of vision with clear color and form. The window was open. The deep blue curtain shook a little, as if there were a breeze. The air in the room shimmered distinctly, as though it contained minute orbs of glass. I saw that countless droplets of water were beading on the pale blue paint of the wall. Seeing the glimmering droplets that had seeped in from the wall's outer surface, I wondered: is it raining outside? Why is it so bright?

The moment I realize I have been sleeping, that I have only dreamed that my eyes were open, I feel no agony. I feel no sense of loss or resignation. As sleep slowly dissipates from my body, I simply turn away from the dream. Simply gaze at the indistinct ceiling, my eyes finally open, and at the collapsed contours of the objects around me. Simply confirm that there is no outside world that I can once more escape to from this dream.

14

Faces

It still doesn't seem real. You, Joachim Gründel, dying at thirty-eight years of age. Like that unfamiliar dream in which I ran my fingertips over every Braille letter and then felt compelled to say I had—somehow—understood.

"I know you aren't able to come from so far away," your mother told me. The funeral would be starting in six hours; she'd deliberately informed me late to ease my mind. I apologized as calmly as I could. She replied that it was all right, and asked if I was getting on okay. I said that I was, and that I would pay her a visit when I returned to Germany. Your mother didn't answer straight away. After a brief silence, she said in a thick voice, "Of course—you are always welcome."

From the Saturday morning when I received that phone call, I've been lying in this bed and looking up at the ceiling. Every time hunger drove me to open the door of the fridge, I was surprised by the distinct outlines of the items inside in that strong illumination. That cold, clearly delineated space seemed a frozen paradise to me, and I lingered with the door open, dragging out the time. Pulling out something simple to eat, I'd sit at the dining table and briefly appease my hunger, then go back and lie down like a patient on bed rest.

.

The window in your room was unusually large and bright.

On afternoons when the room got a lot of light, each of the dozens of model airplanes displayed on the shelf below the window frame gave off a sleek light. While I stood there with my back to you, exclaiming at the exquisite detail of the airplanes, you sat cross-legged on the bed with its blue-and-green checked sheets and carried on talking. Whenever I turned my head and met your gaze, you playfully wrinkled your nose to shift the horn-rimmed glasses up its bridge.

Your brilliantly wide-ranging and freewheeling conversation traversed various topics at length, passing through tunnels and winding routes of allusions and quotes and logical arguments, as befitted someone so well-read. When your words felt drawn out, I would sneak a bite of the wonderful pie your mother had baked and inconspicuously but closely look over the photocopies of old maps on the blue-tinged plaster wall next to the desk, the photographs of planets, the black-and-white miniature drawings of an armadillo, a mammoth, a Neanderthal in profile.

Now and then, and without great tact or care, you took up the topic of my eyes and segued into the inseparable issue of my future. This despite the fact that you were not oblivious of how this privately injured me. You spoke cheerfully: "If I were you, I'd learn Braille ahead of time, to be prepared. And get used to walking around outside on my own with a white cane. I'd get a wonderful, well-trained retriever, and live with it until it died of old age."

In a way, you believed that you had the right to speak to me in this manner. That you'd experienced enough suffering yourself to talk unreservedly about whatever misfortunes the world had to offer. You'd had dozens of operations, major and minor, since you were a newborn, and apparently when you were fourteen you were told you had only six months left to live. You said that all the doctors and nurses were astounded to see you enter university after a period of dogged self-study. You said that I was the first friend you'd made since coming out of hospital.

I remember, distinctly. Your gaunt body, which had shocked me the first time we met. Your forehead, as deeply wrinkled as that of a middle-aged man, though you had been born just seven months ahead of me.

You frowned, furrowing those wrinkles even more deeply, and said, "I have to say . . . if I ever put out a book in my name, I want there to be a Braille edition. I want someone to glide their hand over each letter and each line of the book. That would be . . . I guess real connection, a way for us to really touch. Don't you think?"

You turned your face fully toward mine as if to show that this was not a throwaway comment. I remember your expression, the intent self-awareness of the highly sensitive legible in your face. And those faint blue eyes, your irises clearly visible in the sunlight.

I could tell that you wanted to touch my face then, or for me to touch yours, but I promptly pushed the thought away.

·

Every so often, I think of that Sunday when we climbed the nearby mountain for the first and last time: scrambling over the pale, articular rocks in shorts, taking care not to scratch my calves on the sharp leaves that sprouted from scraggy shrubs, going further up with my palms on my knees for support, resting and wiping away the sweat, guzzling some of the water we'd frozen the night before, munching the black bread we'd wrapped up as a snack, exchanging jokes I can't recall now and idle, pointless laughter; then, seeing the sun begin to set when we still hadn't reached the top, we made our way back down.

"The village where I spent my childhood had rocky mountains like this one," I confided to you then. I told you I came of age looking up at two white peaks called Insubong and Baekundae. That, even to that day, when I thought of my motherland, rather than the bustling city with its population of ten million, I thought of those peaks, which were like a pair of faces.

I recall my words because, rather than responding in your usual jesting and garrulous way, you suffered a fall. You tumbled two or three meters down the sloping path, until a tallish rock brought you up short.

I couldn't believe what was happening. You'd told me that you were completely better now, that you were done reliving the tedious fight with disease that had worn on for twenty years. You'd brandished your cigarettes and defiantly downed glass after glass of beer. I hadn't doubted those words, full of self-confidence, in the slightest.

I remember your stiff face, which looked like that of a stranger. I remember my hands shaking out of fear, the fear of witnessing someone's death for the first time. I remember your closed eyelids, silent and unmoving. I remember descending that steep rocky path with you on my back, my underwear drenched from exertion, pepper-sharp sweat trickling steadily inside my eyelids.

•

Ten days after that descent, you raised your upper body aslant in the hospital's metal bed and said, "You once asked me why I wanted to do philosophy, right? You really want to hear what I think?"

Your glasses were on the bedside table where you'd left them, but you wrinkled your nose all the same.

"You know how they say that, to the Ancient Greeks, virtue wasn't goodness or nobility, but the ability to do a certain thing in the very best way—arete was their word, the capacity for excellence. Well, think about it. Who would be best able to think about life? Someone who faces death at every turn, someone who, for that reason, is inevitably thinking of death, always, necessarily, urgently . . . and wouldn't that effectively mean someone like me possesses the finest arete, at least for contemplation?"

•

This happened on a day many years later, after I'd left you and was traveling alone in Switzerland.

I took a boat from Lucerne harbor and floated through the ice-covered valleys for hours. My initial plan had been to stay on the boat all the way to its final destination—the deepest part of the lake—but I abruptly disembarked at a small city called Brunnen when I saw the two large white rocky peaks flanking the harbor. To my eyes, the left-hand peak resembled Baekundae, and the right resembled Insubong.

Seen from Suyuri, the neighborhood where I grew up, Baekundae rises to the left of Bukhansan, and Insubong to the right. In reality Baekundae is higher, but Insubong looks higher because it stands a little in front. The relative location and slight difference in height between Brunnen's two peaks, even the features of the white rocks and the density of the forests, were reminders of that childhood landscape. Unprepared as I had been to encounter such a familiar sight, I think it came as something of a shock.

As soon as I disembarked at the quay, a young man sitting on an aluminum folding chair in front of a café caught my eye. Pale blond hair and a pleasantly oval face. Baggy dungarees. He didn't resemble you in the slightest, yet he made me think of you.

"What are you eating, is it good?" I asked him as he smiled at me. "Yeah, it's Swiss cheesecake. Since it's Friday," he answered, sticking his thumb up. I went into the café and ordered the same cake, then went outside and sat at the table next to his.

When I asked, "But what's Friday got to do with cheesecake?" he answered, "On Fridays everyone eats cheesecake instead of meat. Not that I'm a deeply religious person or anything . . . it's because Jesus died on a Friday."

The conversation that passed between us was pretty routine. We asked each other where we were born, what we did, what the city was like, where I planned to travel next. I learned that his name was Immanuel and he was an electrician, that he found his job monotonous, that he wanted to travel to Germany and Austria someday, that he'd lived with his mother for ten years after his parents got divorced when he was three, then with his father for the next ten years. He discovered that I was in my second year of "brain-aching" study in Konstanz, which bordered Switzerland, that Bodensee was indeed as beautiful as Lake Lucerne but gloomy in winter as the surrounding towns were constantly shrouded in fog, and that on days when the fog didn't lift until the evening your range of vision was so limited that you had to have your shoulder right up against the outer walls of buildings as you walked along. He seemed somewhat disappointed by the fact that I had never been to Berlin.

I had no desire to look around the small, ordinary town of Brunnen. I was content to sit next to Immanuel and look out at the lake, and to share aimless chat as I ate the cheesecake, which was not at all sweet. The sunlight was dazzling, but the wind off the water was quite sharp.

Around half an hour later the returning boat pulled in, and I parted from Immanuel with a light handshake. We exchanged only names, not email addresses or anything like that. I waved at him as the boat pulled out of the dock, and he waved back at me. The aluminum chair on which I had been sitting, the plate of cheesecake I had left unfinished, grew distant, then faded from view. The figure of Immanuel, who didn't resemble you in the slightest, grew distant, then faded from view. The white peaks that did resemble Baekundae and Insubong grew distant, and eventually, when the boat slipped around a gorge, passed out of view.

Why was I struck by a chill just then? Why does it come back to me so vividly even now, that scene which seemed to tell of a very slow parting, that silence which seemed filled with countless words? As though I were being offered some kind of answer. As though an answer—one that was acutely painful and also a blessing—had already been given to me, and it was up to me to make sense of it.

.

Radiant,
    hazily bright,
    shaded.

I spend three days gazing at the ceiling without my glasses, sensing the minute differences in light intensity that these few expressions cannot render.

It's beyond comprehension.
    You died, and I feel as though everything has fallen away from me.
    You died, that is all,
    and it is as though every single one of my memories is rapidly bleeding, staining, rusting, deteriorating.

.

"The way you do philosophy is too literary," you'd admonish me now and then. "Isn't the place you're trying to arrive at through contemplation simply a kind of literary nirvana?"

I remember the debates we used to have into the late hours. And how, when we were finally done and turned our attention back to the blank wall or the dark curtain, a clean silence would meet us as if it had been waiting all the while. In those days you simply couldn't be beaten. Every question I posed, you would untangle lucidly, whereas your questions always made me lose my way. "Wrong," you would say. "I'm sorry, but what you just said is wrong." As a long discussion was winding down, you'd add, "I do think you're best suited to literature." You were a strict friend in that way, an incredibly exacting teacher, though we were of the same age.

I assumed the teacher's advice was probably correct, but I wasn't able to follow it. I couldn't stand the hours I had to spend reading literary texts. I had no desire to put my trust in a world of wobbly, laxly interlaced sensory perceptions and images, emotions and thoughts.

And yet I couldn't help but become captivated by the things of that world. When Teacher Borchardt explained Aristotle's concept of potentiality, dynamis—"My hair will grey in the future. But that is not present reality. Just as it isn't snowing now, but when winter comes it will snow at least once"—what moved me, simply, was the beautiful melding of those two images. I cannot forget the vision I had then of all our hair—young students' and tall teacher's alike—turning to frost as snow whirled all around us.

It was the same when I read Plato's late works, and was entranced by the question of whether mud, hair, heat-haze, shadows reflected in water, fleeting gestures, have Form. Simply because that wondering was sensually beautiful and touched the electrode inside me that responds to beauty.

•

I remember the theme that was occupying me in those days. The lengthy, futile, forlorn conversations you and I had until the dead of night, about the Forms of darkness, death, dissolution.

You stated that all Forms are beauty and virtue and the sublime. You said this in a calm, sad way, as though you were patiently persuading a younger student. "It simply can't be otherwise, can it? Which is why it has to follow that all Forms are necessarily related to the Form of goodness, do you see? Just as the open plazas of Seoul, Venice, Frankfurt and Mainz all exist on the same day."

Shaking my head, I said, "But what if, supposing there were a Form of dissolution . . . surely it would be a clean, virtuous, sublime dissolution? That is to say, wouldn't the Form of dissolving sleet be sleet that disappears without a trace, cleanly, beautifully, completely?"

You shook your head. "Look at it like this. Death and dissolution are contrary to Forms from the outset. Sleet that melts into mud cannot ever have had a Form."

At your words, the whole ephemeral world lost its color. But the world of sleet that scatters in all directions, eternally unmelting, eternally not settling on the ground, remained spread out before me still like a dark vision.

"Look at it like this," you said again, as though trying to appease me. "In darkness there are no Forms. There is only darkness, a 'minus' darkness. To put it simply, there are no Forms in the sub-zero world. There has to be light, no matter however faint. Without even a feeble light, there is no Form. Don't you get it? It doesn't matter how negligible the beauty, the sublime, but somehow or other there has to be a 'plus' light. Forms of death and dissolution! You may as well be talking of round triangles."

·

That same night, you suddenly asked me, without fear as always, boldly risking the hurt it might cause me, how much of an influence my impending blindness had on my everyday thoughts and feelings.

I stared at your face without answering. At the shadows suspended under your eyes. Your sunken cheeks. Your dark, dead lips.

How should I have answered those hateful words, your cruel question?

I hadn't considered myself through such a stark frame before that day. I'd moved to Germany too late in my teens to have complete command of the German language. However hard I tried, the only subjects where I was able to outstrip my peers were maths and Ancient Greek. It's not unusual for East Asian kids to be good at maths, but Ancient Greek is different. Even my friends who did pretty well at Latin threw up their hands when it came to Greek grammar. Its complicated grammatical system—and the fact that it was a long-dead language—meant Greek felt to me like a safe, quiet room. As I passed more and more time in that room, I became known as the East Asian kid who was surprisingly good at Greek. And it was around then that I began to be drawn to Plato's works as though by a magnetic force.

But was that really how it was? Might it actually have been for the reason you gave that I was drawn to Plato's back-to-front world? Just as, before that, I had been spellbound by Buddhism, which did away with the real world of sensory existence in one fell swoop? That is to say, because I was certain to lose this visible world?

That early dawn, why couldn't I have thrown the same question back at you? Why couldn't I have been brave like you, risked hurting you in the same bold, impertinent way by retorting, "If those are my present circumstances, what influence do *your* circumstances have on *your* thoughts and actions?"

·

During those long hours that I spent with you, the words I actually, desperately wanted to say, more than any other question and answer, more than any quote or allusion or argument, may have been these:

That when the most frail, tender, forlorn parts of us, that is to say our life-breaths, are at some point returned to the world of matter, we will receive nothing in recompense.

That when the time comes for me, I don't see myself remembering the full range of the experiences I'd accumulated up to that point only in terms of beauty.

That it is in this tired, worn context that I understand Plato.

That he himself knew that such beauty does not exist.

And that there is no complete thing, ever. At least in this world.

·

Sometimes I'll recall dream images from that time in my life with unusual clarity.

Snowflakes that melt as soon as they touch late-autumn's still-warm earth.
The vertiginous unfurling of heat-haze in early springtime.

Their faint, muffled presence.
Fragments of a god I never believed in.

Form that is neither born nor extinguished.

The Hwaeom I'd clung to with all I had at fifteen,
which rises behind all beings like dazzling shadows over water,
and blooms forth as thousands of brilliant flowers that encompass the world.

I lie here staring up into the vague whiteness of the emptiness above me, thinking about that world.
I peer at it with eyes wide open.

·

Whereas the things that captivated you then were altogether different:
Physical reality and time.
The world that was born in a heated explosion out of nothingness.

Time's seed in eternal suspension, prior to its unfurling.

Yes, time.

What Borges called a fire that consumes him.

You wanted to touch that riddle with your bare hands, the arrow loosed in a moment that flies forever, the life that, caught within it, stands blazing in the face of extinction.

Eventually, unable to endure your studies, you made your escape.

You swore to me, to your exhausted mother, that you would never be a student again.

I remember your friends, the piercings in their lips, noses, tongues.

And the one friend among them who had unusually sad eyes.

I remember their sorrowful music, how it tore at the heart the louder they played it.

You said to me, No one can understand me unless they also grew up within the benzene smell of hospital wards.

You said, Beauty is only that which is intense, has a vibrant energy.

You said, This thing we call life mustn't ever become something endured.

You said, Dreaming of another world than this is a sin.

And so to you, beauty was the thronging streets.

The tram that stops brimming with simmering sunshine.

The furiously racing heart,

the swelling lungs,

the still-warm lips,

and the fervent rubbing of those lips against another's.

•

Have you lost all of that fire?

Can you really be dead?

Your face immersed in thought.

The deep creases around your mouth.

Your eyes wreathed in smiles.

The way you'd shrug when you didn't want to give an obvious answer.

The first time you embraced me, when I felt the ardent, unconceal-able desire suffusing that gesture, I realized something with spine-tingling clarity:

The sadness of the human body. The human body, with its many indented, tender, vulnerable parts. The forearms. The arm-pits. The chest. The groin. A body born to embrace someone, to desire to embrace someone.

I should have embraced you as hard as I could, at least once before that period of our lives passed us by.

It wouldn't have hurt or harmed me to do so.

I would have withstood it, survived it.

•

Soon I will be unable to distinguish my own reflection from other objects.

All the faces I remember will become fixed, firm and unchang-ing, in my memory as in ice.

————

If you were here, you would advise me without hesitation. You would shrug your shoulders, screw up your nose exaggeratedly and say, "What's the big deal? Learn Braille. Write poetry by boring holes into white paper. Become friends with a golden retriever."

If you hadn't died, would I have touched your face when I saw you again in Germany? Would I have read your forehead, your eyelids, the ridge of your nose, the creases of your cheeks and jaw with my hands?

No, I wouldn't have been able to.

The more time that passed, the more you desired me.

You struggled, unable to endure that desire.

You tore down with your own hands everything that was between us.

I fled far and fast, wounding you deeply.

I resented you.

I couldn't sleep for longing to see the you who was not you.

I yearned like madness only for the you who was not you.

·

Is that lonely body now dead?

Did your body sometimes remember me?

Right at this moment, my body remembers yours.

That brief, agonizing embrace.

Your trembling hands and mildly warm face.

The tears gathered in your eyes.

15

She leans forward.
    Tightens her grip on the pencil.
    Lowers her head further.
    The words evade her grasp.
    Words that have lost lips,
    words that have lost tongue and tooth-root,
    words that have lost throat and breath remain out of reach.
    Like unbodied apparitions, their forms elude touch.

16

ἐπὶ χιόνι ἀνὴρ κατήριπε.
χιὼν ἐπὶ τῇ δειρῇ.
ῥύπος ἐπὶ τῷ βλεφάρῳ.
οὐ ἔστι ὁρᾶν.

αὐτῷ ἀνὴρ ἐπέστη.
οὐ ἔστι ἀκούειν.

A person lies prone in the snow.
Snow in their throat.
Earth in their eyes.
Seeing nothing.

A person stands next to them.
Hearing nothing.

17

Darkness

A bird has just flown into the building. A titmouse, smaller than a young child's fist. It starts to bump its head against the concrete wall and against the railing of the stairs that lead up to the first floor, crying urgently, as if, having just flown in, it nonetheless cannot find the way out.

The woman steps in through the entrance and quietly stops in her tracks. She watches as the bird strikes its head against the wall once again, then she turns back. Opens the closed half of the double glass door. Says, from a place deeper than throat and tongue, *Come on out now.*

To encourage the bird, she gently thumps her bag against the wall. The bird clearly takes this as a threat. It flies straight down into the darkness of the stairs that lead to the basement, hides itself under the railing and doesn't budge.

You can't hide there. Come on out now.

She draws back two steps and hears a frail chirping, ppi-i ppi-i, as though the bird has lowered its guard. She takes a step forward and the sound abruptly stops. She looks out of the open doors. Summer trees, their trunks touched with white, are steeped in the evening glow. A taxi with its fog lights on pulls up in front of the glass doors.

The man gets out of the taxi. He is wearing a plain white cotton shirt and dark grey cotton trousers. In order not to trip on the dark steps leading up to the entrance, as soon as he gets out of the taxi he switches on a small flashlight. He turns it off upon entering the building's illuminated interior, adjusts the shoulder strap of his heavy-looking bag and walks over to the woman. He hesitates, then asks in a low voice, "What are you looking at?"

The man leans forward, toward the black living thing beneath the stair railing that the woman is peering at. It moves slightly in the darkness. He switches on his flashlight and shines it in that direction. Is it a rat? A kitten? He can't make it out.

What he can make out is the tension in the woman's breathing. He realizes that this is the first time he has heard her make any kind of sound. She has her hair tied tightly back. The stray strands below her ears quiver in time with her inhales and exhales. The man wishes he could see her properly. The overhead lights are not bright enough for him to make out the expression on the woman's face, and he can't very well shine the flashlight at her.

As he wonders whether he should try to sign to her again, the sound of the woman's breathing grows distant. The black short-sleeved blouse and black trousers, the glimpsed face, neck and arms, grow distant. The sound of low-heeled shoes rings out distinctly on the stone stairs like punctuation marks. The man stands and strains to listen to that sound, which continues without a pause all the way to the second-floor corridor. Listening to the footsteps pull wordlessly, endlessly away, he wonders what feelings they are stirring up in him, wonders when it was he had felt this conflicted.

The man takes a step to follow the woman, but stops when he hears a ppi-i ppi-i sound. He looks toward the bottom of the stairs, and the black object that had been lying motionless hops two, three steps up from the basement. He shines the flashlight at it, but it curls up again and becomes deathly still. Only then does he guess that it is a bird.

"Come out. You shouldn't be here."

His voice echoes in the dark corridor. He turns his head and looks at the trees outside the front entrance. The evening is rapidly deepening and the outlines of trunks and limbs appear almost black.

He hesitates, then opens his bag and pulls out a thick textbook. He rolls it up and holds it in one hand, then, shining the flashlight with the other hand, cautiously descends the stairs. He isn't planning to go down more than three steps. The bird still doesn't move an inch. He stoops to usher the bird in the right direction with the book, but the bird flaps up at him all of a sudden, chirping sharply. Trying to avoid the bird flying at his face, he loses his footing on the stairs. Drops the flashlight. The bird bangs its head against the wall, the railing. It flies at him again. His glasses fall off. Hearing a fluttering sound just behind his ear, he wraps his arms around his face and staggers. Twice, three times, he steps on his glasses, cracking the lenses. Shunted underfoot, they tumble down to the bottom of the stairs. Flapping its wings with all its strength, the bird darts toward the glass doors. Dashes its head against the concrete wall, the tin mailboxes.

He is sitting on the dark stairs. Everything is black, mauled. He gropes the stairs with trembling hands, searching for his glasses. Far below him, how far he cannot judge, the flashlight lies in a foggy halo of light.

"Is anyone there?"

His voice is hoarse, and doesn't come out well.

"Is anyone there?"

He brings his wristwatch right up to his eyes and squints at the yellow-green luminous hands. He can hardly make them out. Probably around a quarter past eight. It is the final week in July, the Thursday before the peak of the summer holiday. Friday's class has been canceled, and the part-time admin said she would leave the classroom door open and take off early for her hometown. The middle-aged man with the nine-to-six job had let him know in advance that he would be absent today. Which meant that only the woman, the postgrad and the philosophy student would be there right now, in the second-floor classroom. The woman is someone who cannot help him. The other two are the types to wait patiently for a good half-hour for the lecturer to appear, chatting about this and that.

He begins to feel his way over the stairs with both hands. When he has felt all along one step, he lowers himself down to the next, still in a seated position. Luckily, his fingers find his bag not far away. Opening the front zip and fumbling around inside, he discovers that he has forgotten his mobile. This afternoon, a letter he'd sent to Germany a month ago had been returned, and, though he'd only briefly become distracted as he placed it on his desk and let his thoughts wander, it had still made him late. He can't recall having collected his phone as he rushed out of the door after only a quick shave.

After fixing the bag diagonally across his chest so that it wouldn't fall off again, he recommences groping the stairs. He can feel only dirt and dust, and small hard fragments of things he cannot identify. Whenever he comes across a few sharp fragments, he gives that area a thorough going-over, but he can't be sure if it's glass from his lenses.

On his hands and bottom, he lowers himself toward the center of what seems like a diffuse pool of light deep under the sea. Before anything else, he needs to get his hands on that flashlight. As his palms scrape over the stair, he groans. He has found his glasses. They are completely broken. At the sharp, warm sensation of blood flowing from the fingertips of his right hand, he bites down on the inside of his lower lip. He fumbles his uninjured left hand over every inch of the bent frames, the now-empty spaces where the lenses have shattered.

How much time has gone by?

He hears no sign of anyone.

Whether it has long flown out the doors or died from battering its head, even the bird is silent.

On such a still evening as this, wouldn't he be able to hear, even faintly, the two male students talking, especially the postgrad's loud, resonant voice?

If they haven't shown up, that means the only person in the second-floor classroom is the woman.

He thinks of her sitting silently in the empty classroom, and shuts his eyes tightly. The puddle of light disappears, but the darkness that flickers and wavers behind his eyelids is almost the same as when he had his eyes open.

He cannot call out to the woman for help.

The woman cannot hear.

Eventually he opens his eyes. He runs his left hand over the next stair down, preparing to lower himself further toward the pooled light. Just then, he hears footsteps ring out in the corridor of the floor above.

Making an effort to keep his hands away from the broken glass this time, he begins to falter his way upward on hands and knees. He's certain. It's the same footsteps as before. He pounds the metal railing with his fist. Swings his heavy bag against it over and over again. If she cannot hear, perhaps she will sense these vibrations.

"Help me," he shouts, even as he's convinced it's useless. Eventually the sound of footsteps draws toward the basement stairs.

He is unable to identify the moving darkness, the darkness that overlies the darkness. All he can sense is that the footsteps have stopped somewhere close by, that there is a faint sound of someone breathing, that the person is approaching. He opens his eyes as wide as he can and looks toward the direction of the sound.

"Can you hear me?

Is there no one else upstairs?

My glasses are broken. My sight is very bad."

"Would you call someone?

I need to get a taxi, before the optician's closes."

"Can you hear me?"

A faint apple scent reaches his nose. Two cold, agile hands slide under his armpits. Those hands guide him to his feet. He struggles to tread securely over the floor he cannot see. Leaning on the arms of a person he cannot see, he climbs the stairs one step at a time. Each time he loses his footing, the arms supporting him regain their strength.

The luminosity of the darkness is changing. Now he can discern that the stairs have ended, and that they are approaching the front entrance, where the lights are on. The contours of things reappear, dim and black. The grey that he guesses are the mailboxes, the white section of wall, the overwhelming darkness that must be what lies outside the double doors.

The woman has one arm across his back; her other hand supports his wrist. The humid breeze hits him. They are standing in front of the wide-open glass doors. The vague outline of the woman's face and arm is dimly guessed at. He carelessly wipes his bleeding hand on his shirt. The smashed, warped glasses he's been clutching all this time fall to his feet. Are the red splotches continuously materializing down there his blood? He bends to pick up his glasses. He cannot reach them. Moistening his dry lips with the tip of his tongue, he says to the woman, "My wallet is in my bag. There's enough for the taxi fare. If we go downtown, we'll be able to find an optician's. I need new glasses."

18

Each time there is a dip in the pavement, she signals by tugging at his arm. Each time he lifts one foot into the air and then puts it down, she can feel his anxiety. Once they've made their way out of the dark alleys, she stands in front of the pedestrian crossing of the two-lane road, her arms still supporting the Greek teacher, and looks around in all directions.

They have to find a pharmacy. The one opposite has its shutters down. There isn't much traffic here, making it hard to hail a taxi. The local buses arrive less frequently once the evening rush hour is over. As she used to do whenever her child was taken ill, she coolly and quickly arranges the order of business. There is a deep cut in his right hand; dust and dirt cover the gash. She had bound his wrist with her handkerchief in order to lessen the bleeding; already more than half the handkerchief is soaked with blood. Small fragments of glass might be embedded in the cut, so she had been wary of applying pressure to stop the bleed or wiping the blood too thoroughly.

She looks at his profile. She looks at the darkness of the tarmac that his unsteady gaze is moving over. His face looks unfamiliar without his glasses, probably because of his eyes, which are larger than she had guessed them to be, and the expression on his face as he struggles to conceal his terror and bewilderment.

She takes hold of his uninjured left hand and draws it to her. Breathing in, she uses the tip of her trembling index finger to write distinctly on his palm.

First
　to the
　hospital

19

A Conversation in Darkness

"Would you switch on the desk lamp?
The incandescent over the table is better than the ceiling light.
It's actually harder to see if it's too bright."

She removes her shoes and enters the room. It is a frugally decorated studio. There is a metal-framed single bed and a mattress with a dark blue cover, next to a desk made of knotty cryptomeria and a bookcase about a meter wide. Plain mugs, brass rice bowls and small dishes are neatly arranged on the rack above the sink. A small, slim fridge for single-person homes stands next to it.

She walks into the room as far as the desk, where five or six books lie open with their corners overlapping. She switches on the light-brown shaded desk lamp that sits next to a magnifying glass. As she returns to the entrance, he reaches out his hand and feels along the wall. He lowers the switch for the fluorescent ceiling light she had turned on a moment ago. He flicks the switch below that one, and a yellow light falls from the incandescent lamp suspended over the kitchen table.

"You don't have to hold on to me now.
 Ah, you've put my bag down here.
 It's fine. I just need to know where it is.
 I won't bump into or trip over things here, you needn't worry."

She had grabbed his bag from the spot by the shoe cupboard where she'd left it; now she puts it back down. Her black blouse is damp from the humidity that has persisted into the night. Her hair, which has come loose and lies disheveled around her shoulders, is also full of sweat. His white shirt is completely soaked at the back. The scattered drops of blood over his chest have now dried dark. His tightly bandaged right hand hangs at his side. Their arms and faces are slick with sweat.

"Would you care to sit on the bench by the window?
 It's the coolest spot in the room.
 I actually sleep there when it's very hot."

She walks over to the wooden bench, long enough to lie down on if you curl up a little. She sets her bag on it instead of sitting down herself. Standing against the chair, she watches him walk directly over to the bed without stumbling, and sit down on it. A little while ago, in the taxi, he had guided them with similar ease. "After the crossroads, please take the first alley on the left. It's the building right after the By the Way convenience store." When the taxi stopped, he asked her in a low voice, "Is it the building right after the By the Way?" In lieu of an answer, she had briefly laid her hand on his arm.

"I'm sorry, I don't have a fan.
  I try not to accumulate belongings."

As though he has no idea what else to say now that they are sitting at a distance, he looks ill at ease. He gazes over in her direction, then raises his unbandaged left hand and points at the fridge.

"Would you like a glass of water?
  I have bottled water in the fridge.
  No, stay where you are.
  I'll get it.
  Though I won't be able to pour it into a cup.
  My right hand being as it is."

He stands up from the bed and moves over to the fridge. Opens the door with his left hand, reaches into the top compartment for two small bottles of mineral water and tucks them under his right arm. She moves to come and help.

"No, don't trouble yourself.
  I can do it."

He approaches her with careful footsteps. With his left hand he removes one of the bottles from under his right arm and holds it out to her. Still standing, she takes it.

"If I had my glasses, I could have made some iced coffee.

I have a younger sister who rarely has a good word to say about her brother.

She does approve of my iced coffees, though.

She's in Germany now.

She sings in a vocal ensemble.

She's had the longest career of the sopranos."

He sits on the bed, she on the bench, each of them holding a bottle of water. She looks at the veneer-wood flooring, at the shadows the furniture casts on it. When she looks up at the ceiling, she sees their two black shadows on its rice-color wallpaper, swollen surprisingly huge.

She is suddenly aware of the chirring of insects coming from outside the window. It is similar to the sound she hears on the narrow street along the motorway to her house. All that's missing is the shriek of vehicles that slices into her ears like blades on ice.

•

"This feels strange.

Earlier, when we were at the hospital, I didn't mind talking to myself like this . . .

Perhaps because you would occasionally write answers on my palm."

He extends his left hand into the air, then quickly pulls it back on to his lap. Three vertical lines resembling the hanja for "stream" form between his eyebrows as he tries to bring something of the blur in front of him into focus.

"In the emergency ward, I could hear a lot of different sounds simultaneously.

An elderly woman seemed to have burned herself.

A child around four, no, three years old, was crying its heart out.

Someone was yelling incoherently in the background.

I heard a doctor speak very rudely to a patient, and in banmal at that."

She recalls those people; she had seen each of them with her eyes. An old woman with grey-streaked hair had the burns. She'd said a medical pad she was using on her knee had suddenly burst into flames. A three-year-old child had had the top joint of his index finger severed. The young mother had brought the grain-sized tip wrapped in a gauze cloth, but the nurse had told her, "I'll put this on ice for you, but you have to go to a big hospital. We don't have any doctors here who can do the surgery." As her exhausted child clung to her back, the mother, unaware of her own tears, had nodded vigorously. "I understand, quickly, please get it ready quickly." While that hasty exchange was going on, a middle-aged woman's wails could be heard coming from the treatment room near the entrance, where she was having her stomach pumped. Eu-uh-uh. Eu-uh-uh. It was impossible to make out the words, given the tube inserted into her throat. A young doctor had been incredibly offensive: he'd sneeringly said to the patient, "See what you got yourself into?"

·

"I never imagined I would end up indebted like this."

She unscrews the lid of the water bottle and takes a sip. Rests for a moment, then takes another sip. She listens to the chirring outside the window, listens to the abrupt silences that turn out to be caesurae.

"I don't know how I can repay you."

He frequently lapses into reticences, as though finding it difficult to carry on the conversation by himself.

"They don't know at the academy that my eyesight is this bad. It wasn't strictly necessary for me to inform them, so I never mentioned it. And so—"

He breaks off. She looks at the telegraph pole outside the dark window. The densely tangled black cables keep their peace, concealing the high-voltage current that runs through them. He likely wanted to say, And so, I would be grateful if you don't tell anyone. Only to realize it was a pointless request to make of her.

"Up until now, I've been able to get by somehow or other as long as I have my glasses.
    What's to come is less certain."

She feels that his pauses and the insects' stridulations are forming a delicate syncopation. Ppirrk, ppirk, a keen sound, like a high note dragged out by an inexpert bow, follows his voice. Now a hush abruptly wedges itself in again, and this time the shaky string note is the first to sound.

·

"When I first understood that my eyesight would at some point worsen significantly, I asked my mother if everything around me would go pitch-black . . .

When really it was my father I should have asked, as it was his side that had the bad eyes. Father, grandfather and great-grandfather all.

But my father was an indifferent man.

And my mother someone who endeavored to answer any question as best she could."

She holds her breath, then slowly releases it. For the face of her own mother, as it looked at the end, has risen up in her mind. During those final thirteen hours, her mother had breathed sluggishly, eyes and mouth half open. Her elder brother and his wife, who had emigrated to Argentina around a decade previously, had caught a flight via Los Angeles and were somewhere above the Pacific Ocean. She whispered into her mother's ear without rest. The hospice staff had advised her to recount stories to her mother, had said her hearing was alive even if she seemed unconscious.

As for which story to tell, she didn't have a choice in the matter: it had to be of the summer afternoon long ago when her whole family had played water games. The yard of their old hanok house, the ground covered in a thin layer of cement. The transparent stream of water shooting from the hose. Her father and elder brother, collecting the water in a metal bucket with swift movements. Herself at seven years old, soaked from head to toe, running about yelling. Her mother, screaming with laughter like an impish young woman, as though twenty years had suddenly fallen from her, hurling bowls of water at her husband and children.

She moistened her mother's black lips with a wet flannel and tilted the water bottle to her own dry lips, whispering all the while. When she thought to herself that she couldn't carry on any longer, she whispered faster. When she eventually fell silent, it happened. A birdlike thing abruptly departed the body, and the body was no longer her mother. *Mum, where have you gone?* The question lodged itself in her throat as she sat there blankly, not even thinking to close the body's eyelids.

.

"And my mother told me no, she said it would be both bright and dark. That everything would just get very hazy.

I could make a rough guess as to what that would be like, as, with my right eye closed, everything I saw with my bad left eye was already quite blurry.

My little sister heard this and ran into the kitchen.

She rummaged around in the cupboard for a translucent plastic bag and held it up against her eyes.

She said, 'Well, there's the sofa and there's the bookcase.'

'That's white and that's orange.'

'Look, I can walk around without tripping over anything.'

Our mother snatched the plastic bag out of my fascinated sister's hand with a withering look."

———————

He tilts the bottle to his lips. Happily gulps down the water. She sees the soft generosity that his face reveals, the tenderness occasioned by remembering his flesh and blood. His dark, hardened face relaxes. Brightens a little.

"Our mother was strict and intimidating.
    She didn't tolerate anyone teasing me about my sight.
    But my little sister had been truly relieved for me in that moment.
    She'd just discovered that her father's near-future and her brother's distant-future wouldn't be as awful as she'd thought.
    But my mother was too serious a person to understand that."

She listens to him without giving any indication that she is listening. She soon realizes that something, perhaps something akin to a bird, is living within the contours of his face, and that the warmth of it awakens an immediate pain in her.

.

"Are you listening?"

He is uneasy all of a sudden, clutching the half-empty bottle in his left, unbandaged hand. He reaches out and sets it down on the desk next to the bed.

"Don't you have to go?
    Won't your family be worried?"

Her face darkens briefly. She has remembered playing hide-and-seek with her cousins when she was young. At the house of her father's younger brother, in their tiny village full of people with the same family name. She had been blindfolded with a handkerchief, and her cousins hid. Stretching out her hands to grab a presence that felt just out of reach, she heard muffled laughter. After searching the empty air for a while, she suddenly felt a chill and stopped short. She removed the covering from her eyes and examined the rooms, the doors of which had been flung wide open, and discovered that all her cousins had disappeared outside.

"Are you listening over there?"

The light goes out in his face too. The warm bird curls into a ball and hides. She wavers, then carefully moves her feet and knees to make her presence known. Sets the water bottle she has been holding down on the chair.

.

He hesitates before starting on the next story. Fixes his gaze in the direction of her face, which he cannot see.

"When I left my mother and sister in Germany to come to Seoul, I booked a one-way ticket. I did consider getting a round-trip ticket with an open return date, but for some reason I didn't want to."

He moistens his lips with the tip of his tongue. He leaves long pauses between one sentence and the next. Similar to how someone writing in the dark tries to leave a wide margin between lines so the sentences written above and below won't overlap.

"The plane flew eastward, eastward . . . on the westerlies. Each time I looked out of the window, we seemed to be riding on an enormous arrow. But an arrow speeding not toward any target but toward what lay outside it."

Slowly, carefully, she moves her foot to make a sound.

"Half the passengers were Germans, and the other half were Koreans; a Korean air hostess, the only one, asked me in Korean, 'What would you like to drink?' And I laughed. I realized that on that flight, I was no longer conspicuous."

He picks up the water bottle and wets his lips.

"When we first moved to Frankfurt, my mother was constantly on edge. As foreigners, especially as conspicuous East Asians, she was adamant that we should not make any missteps. It was a compulsive, obsessive anxiety. When we went out on the weekends, she would squabble with my father over the most trivial thing.

'And what happens if we drive down and there's no Kasse at the exit? So what if it's far? We know for sure there's one on the first floor. So let's go back and make sure our parking fee's all paid up . . . Listen, we're foreigners here. They'll think we were trying to get past without paying. Well, I'm saying what if there's no Kasse at the exit . . . No, it's not okay. Why take the risk?' "

A bitter smile rises to his lips.

"Compared with my father, who went on brusquely repeating that it was fine and she shouldn't worry, my mother's fretting did seem excessive, but, looking back at it now, for the most part she had it right. There were instances here and there of discrimination and unfair treatment, though they weren't always explicit. At the school my sister and I attended; at the German companies and government offices my father dealt with. Looks of barely concealed, icy disdain and contempt that couldn't be called anything but a racial gaze."

When his silences become drawn out, she makes a small movement to signal her presence. Sweeps her hand across the armrest of the wooden chair or sweeps up her hair, then becomes still again.

"Our mother was permanently exhausted. After we moved to Mainz, so that she could provide for us when our father no longer could, she opened a shop selling Asian groceries, and we practically never saw her smile at home. She'd grumble to us, 'How is it, each time you meet a stranger's eye in this country, you're supposed to smile? I'm done with smiling. I won't do it anymore. Let me live as I want. I'd rather not smile, at least not in my own home. But don't mistake that for anger—I may not smile, but that doesn't mean I'm angry.' "

It takes only a small movement to make her shadow on the ceiling lurch, magnified. The slightest tremor in her face and hands sets the shadow astir as though dancing.

"As a teenager, I myself struggled with smiling. Having to act all cheerful and confident; always having to be ready with a greeting or a smile was exhausting. Sometimes simply saying hello and smiling felt like labor. Then there were days when I felt I couldn't endure a second more of people smiling just for the sake of it. And so I'd risk being stereotyped as another oriental martial-arts thug and pull my cap down low, stuff my fists in my pockets and walk around with the most unfriendly expression I could manage."

Their magnified shadows on the ceiling suddenly stop moving. Soundlessly, firmly cleaving to their black borders, they remain apart.

"Eventually the plane landed at Incheon Airport, and I disembarked with a smile, a smile I had practiced and honed for so long it was by then as good as my own. When my body came in close proximity to someone else's, I felt like saying 'Excuse me' in German. When my eyes met someone else's, I felt like smiling. But as I walked out of Arrivals, it hit me. Shouldering my way through the crowd of Koreans waiting for their family and friends, I realized I wasn't conspicuous, not here, not anymore. And that I was finally, safely back in the folds of a culture where people aren't expected to exchange smiles or greetings with every passing stranger.

I couldn't understand why this caused such a wrenching sense of solitude in me then."

•

She feels the chirring outside the window as a needle piercing the hush of the room. Boring countless imperceptible holes into a charged silence that is as taut as fabric caught in a tambour.

The shadows remain impassive. She stifles even her breathing. His face is pallid, frozen.

•

"That reminds me of our first winter in Germany, when the three of us, minus our father, went on a train journey to Italy."

His monologue speeds up in increments. As when a page is marred by hasty scribbles done in the dark. Line overlaying line, ink overlaying ink, memory overlaying memory.

"I don't remember much. Not clearly, not anything else we saw in Italy. Not the artwork, the churches, the food. The only thing I can't forget are the catacombs."

•

"It was a city of the dead . . .
     Each passage forked off in three different directions.
     The stories about the tourist who lost their way and died of starvation made sense then.
     The walls of the stone chambers were made up of tombs shaped like different-sized drawers.

The Korean tour guide accompanying us on our trip asked, 'Can anyone guess why there are no remains to be seen in these tombs?'

My sister with her carrying voice answered, 'Because they've been taken to a museum?' The guide said that was incorrect.

'Someone stole them?' another tourist suggested, and the guide again shook her head.

'They're all here,' the guide said, almost proudly.

'If you did a chemical analysis of the earth that lies in these tombs, right here in front of you, you'd find large amounts of calcium and phosphorus.

After thousands of years, this is what a person's bones become.' "

She turns to look out of the window. In the darkness, the electric cables remain snarled. Sunk in an untroubled stillness, even as they allow voices, images, countless blinking letters and characters to flow into the high-voltage current.

"I thought I might vomit. Out of terror at the earth in front of me. Afraid it would get on my body. But I couldn't run. It was too dark. Everywhere I looked the same three-pronged passage lay before me."

I thought I might vomit, she mumbles from a place deeper than tongue or throat.

Some months ago, she had spent several days vomiting at two-hour intervals. This was right after she'd lost custody of her child. When she brought her son home a week later, she somehow managed to make a favorite dish of his, omu-rice, then she herself ate nothing but cabbage for the rest of the evening. Either puréed in the blender or steamed in a pan. There was nothing else her insides would tolerate.

"You're going to turn into a rabbit, Mum," her child said. "Your whole body will go green." She laughed along, then went to the toilet to vomit again. Rinsing out her mouth, soured with stomach acid, she came out of the toilet and teasingly asked, "Why don't rabbits turn green? When all they eat is grass?" "Because," her child said, "rabbits eat carrots too!" Fighting down the nausea, she laughed.

.

"Talking by myself like this and at such length, I'm strangely reminded of that moment.

Of how we were gathered there, our bodies still holding all their warmth, inside that enormous tomb where thousands of what were once such bodies had entirely disintegrated away, even the bones."

Ink overlays ink, memory overlays memory, bloodstain overlays bloodstain. Serenity over serenity, smile over smile, bears down.

.

"I'm exhausted . . ."

He is silent for a while.

"I feel I may not wake up for several days if I sleep now."

.

He is feeling for something with his hands, teeth clenched. He goes over the same spot twice. As she does when she moves her hands over the ice of silence. When one layer of ice melts, a three-pronged road will be waiting. And beneath another layer of ice, another three-pronged road, and beneath yet another, thicker layer of ice, another road . . . branching off, endlessly.

"There was this one time when I really didn't wake up for days.
    Someone had hit me in the face with a block of wood.
    Not some unknown assailant.
    It was someone I knew very well.
    My glasses shattered, and I was badly cut.
    I still have the scar."

Her gaze touches the faint line that runs from the corner of his eye to the corner of his mouth. She realizes, now that the night has grown as deep as it will get, the tenuous stridulation is about to cease for good. There is only the black darkness swaying in and out of countless windows flung open in the sweltering night, and in and out of countless finely meshed mosquito screens, like ghosts.

"I was completely unconscious for some time, and when I woke up I was in a hospital room.

A shared room, but the other two beds were empty.

I looked over at the darkened windows and thought, 'Is it about to get lighter now or darker?'"

.

That instant, the memory of a long-lost word rises up in her, cut in half, and she tries to grab hold of it. She had learned that, in times past, there had been a word, a Hanja word beginning with 呼, ho, by which people had referred to the half-light just after the sun sets and just before it rises. A word that means having to call out in a loud voice, as the person approaching from a distance is too far away to be recognized, to ask who they are. A word whose derivation is similar to the Western expression "The hour of dogs and wolves," a word beginning with ho ... This eternally incomplete, eternally unwhole word stirs deep within her, never reaching her throat.

"My mother and sister had just come into the ward; they took one look at me and cried out.

My sister ran off to call the nurse.

A junior doctor with unkempt hair, worn out by her day, caught up with me.

By then the dark blue light had turned black."

When she was young, she had woken from a long nap and crawled on her knees to the door. It was the door that led to the dark old-style kitchen. She went down the stairs on her bottom, and, when she landed on the kitchen floor, she saw her mother squatting in front of the paraffin cooker, making black beans in soy sauce. In vague confusion she asked, "Mum, is it tomorrow?" Her mother burst out laughing. The darkness permeating every corner of the kitchen was that of night. It was a deeper, more solid darkness than the dark of dawn. And on some level she had sensed this, which is why she'd wondered if it was "tomorrow."

"The doctor told me I had been unconscious for three days.

And that no one knew why, given that the external trauma had not been serious."

A faint, oddly melancholy smile forms on his face.

"That was the first and the last time I slept so deeply, without even dreaming."

Quietly, as water stains a dry board, the smile spreads across his face.

·

In time . . .

his voice wanes.

I will see only when I dream.

At a certain point, he seems to have forgotten whom he is speaking to. He seems to be addressing someone who isn't here.

•

"A rose."

"The inner red of a watermelon, blooming like a flower, when you split it open."

"The night of Buddha's Birthday."

"Snowflakes."

"The face of a woman long gone."

"I won't be waking from a dream and opening my eyes;

the world is what will close when I wake from a dream."

Fatigued, she closes her eyes for a long moment before opening them again. That she is here, now, does not feel real. When she closes her eyes again, her consciousness tries to ebb away from her waking life. If she were to open her eyes now, she might see the ceiling of her own living room. She might have been asleep all this time, curled up in her usual spot on the living room sofa.

Several hours ago, during the thirty or so minutes when she had waited in the empty classroom for the lesson to begin, she had felt a similar confusion. The Greek lecturer, who always arrived early and waited for the students, hadn't appeared for some reason. Nor had any of the other students, not the middle-aged man who favored the spot behind the pillar, nor the postgrad near the window who liked to expel the sharp-edged Greek words through his teeth, nor the young philosophy student who looked at her with blinking, curious eyes.

The blackboard, the platform in front of the blackboard, the students' desks—all stood empty. The two fans were unmoving, angled toward opposite walls as though avoiding each other. The empty desks and chairs, where the students usually stood or sat lively and animated, chatting with each other when they weren't talking on their phones, burrowed into her eyes, charged with a strange aching sensation. She had squeezed her eyes tight. Time as it was for her seemed out of joint with how it was for everyone else. Sharply dislocated, like a fault line in a rocky crag, so that the two temporalities might never again coincide. Blankly listening to the muffled sound of traffic, she had packed her textbook, notebook and cloth pencil case back into her bag. Leaving the lights on in the silent classroom, she had walked out into the dark corridor, her shoes ringing out unusually loudly against the floor.

·

"Are you listening over there?"

His voice sounds transformed, like something coming out of a speaker muffled by damp air.

With her eyes closed, she doubts whether the voice is that of the Greek lecturer. Does it match the voice she's heard these many months in the desolate classroom? Had that voice been so frail, so tremulous?

•

Do you ever wonder at the strangeness of it?

That our bodies have eyelids and lips,

that they can at times be made to close from the outside,
  and at other times to lock fast from within.

•

Laboriously raising her heavy eyelids, she recalls, as if in a brief sleep, the alleyway in front of her old house, where the sun used to set. She and her young mother had been on their way to see her mother's parents. "Let's stop at the market and buy tangerines," she heard her mother say. She had been struggling to zip up her coat, but at these words, bright orange tangerines appeared before her eyes. She was amazed they weren't real, that she wasn't actually seeing them, when they looked so delicious. She hurriedly thought of something else—trees—but the same thing happened. It was like magic. In front of her lay only the darkening alleyway and the seemingly endless stretch of concrete wall, and yet she was quite clearly looking at a tree. The shapes of letters she'd only just learned began to superimpose themselves over the tree. 나무. Saying the word out loud, she laughed to herself. Namu. Namu. *Tree.*

•

"Does it sound strange to you, all this I'm saying?"

She opens her eyes and looks at his face. She sees the old scar and the new smudge of dust from when he ran his hand over it earlier. She closes her eyes again. Sees the boyish face she'd seen in him moments ago rise up, intact, in that same magic she'd experienced as a child.

"If you don't mind, there's something I'd like to ask. Truly, I hope you won't be offended . . ."

His voice falls.

"That is, have you always . . . have you always been unable to speak?"

•

The ceiling is covered with plain rice-colored wallpaper, and the books in the bookcase are completely still. The sound of crickets has died away. The only things bruising the silence in the shadowy room are the engine sounds coming from afar. Wind enters through the open window. A sodden wind, like a wet towel. She feels the urge to pass a cold towel over her face, which is sticky now that the sweat has dried. The urge to wipe away the new smudge on his face.

"What sort of work do you do?"

•

She stares at his searching eyes, his tensed lips, his jaw and the edges of his cheeks, where a bluish shadow has begun to emerge as the night wears on. As though, hidden within the strokes and dots that make up his face, there are marks or pictographs that she needs to decipher. As though she has only to render that face as a drawing with a few strokes for some quiet words to be revealed.

Early in the spring of her second year in high school, she had written a few poems with the title "Pictograph." She wrote in the hope of conveying an understated humor. The small "a" of the roman alphabet as an exhausted person with their head and shoulders slumped forward. The Hanja for "light," 光, gwang, a shrub rooting down underground as overground it rises toward the light. The echoic 우우우, woo-oo-oo, the sound of rumbling shouts, a row of raindrops along a window ledge rolling off as one, or tears that well up and trickle down from under one's lashes. Bright, quiet, naive poems she never showed to anyone.

But the poems she wrote sometime later were different. Little by little, her words began to falter and trail off, finally breaking into fragmented units, or decaying into formlessness like flesh that had fallen away.

·

"Why are you studying Greek?"

Off her guard, she looks down at her left wrist. Beneath the dark purple hairband, which is damp with sweat, the old scar is also clammy. She will not remember. And, if she must remember, if it is absolutely unavoidable, she will not feel anything.

Eventually, without feeling, as though remembering a distant acquaintance, she recalls that day. "You're insane," the person had spat at her from the dark, when she regained consciousness. "All this time, I let a crazy bitch look after my child." Short-tongued and shallow-throated words, loose words, words that slipped and slashed and stabbed, metallic, filled her mouth. Before they fell woo-soo-soo out of her mouth like the splintered pieces of a razor blade, before she was able to spit them out, they had first wounded her.

·

"That day, what did you write in Greek in your notebook?"

She brushes her fingers over her lips as though touching a huge abraded saw. As though remembering a long-atrophied organ, she searches in her mind for the route by which words had once shakily gushed out.

She knows that no single specific experience led to her loss of language.

Language worn ragged over thousands of years, from wear and tear by countless tongues and pens. Language worn ragged over the course of her life, by her own tongue and pen. Each time she tried to begin a sentence, she could feel her aged heart. Her patched and repatched, dried-up, expressionless heart. The more keenly she felt it, the more fiercely she clasped the words. Until all at once, her grip slackened. The dulled fragments dropped to her feet. The saw-toothed cogs stopped turning. A part of her, the place within her that had been worn down from hard endurance, fell away like flesh, like soft tofu dented by a spoon.

.

Could not be reconciled.

The things not to be reconciled with were everywhere.

In the body of a homeless person, found dead on a park bench beneath several layers of newspaper on a bright spring day. In the dull eyes of people riding the subway late at night, all looking off in different directions as they stood shoulder to sweat-gummed shoulder. In the line of vehicles on the motorway, their endless trail of taillights in torrential rain. In the procession of days, each day nicked and torn open by numerous skate blades. In human bodies, so easily crushed. In the exchange of foolish, clipped jokes that are meant to make us forget all. In the words we press on to paper so as to not forget a single thing. And in the foul stench of the gas bubbling up out of those words before we know it.

Occasionally, after a long period of solitude or illness, in the early hours before dawn or late into the night, extraordinarily clean, serene words did flow out of her, quite unexpectedly, as though she were speaking in tongues, but she could not believe that this was proof of her reconciliation.

.

Fatigue is like a heady intoxication dulling her thoughts.

His voice sounds like something in a dream, arriving as if from a great distance in broken fragments.

———————

There are moments when I think I get it, when I feel I understand him.

There are moments when I want to stop talking.

She makes an effort to look at his face. To look steadily into his unfocused eyes.

When I write with white chalk on the dark green blackboard, I am terrified.

My own writing, and yet, from more than ten centimeters away, I can't see it.

When I read out something I've memorized, I am terrified.

The phonemes my tongue and teeth and throat so calmly articulate terrify me.

The silence of the space into which my voice travels terrifies me.

Words that are irrevocable, that can't be taken back, that are aware of so much more than myself, terrify me.

.

It occurs to her that she can no longer tell whose words it is she is hearing. Inside this horrible fatigue, in this horribly dim, sedate room, everything feels like an apparition. She has heard nothing. She has glimpsed the inner life of nothing and no one.

There are times when it feels like I'm moving through a fog.

Like on winter days in that city when early-morning fog would roll in from the lake and smother the town well into the evenings.

Like the nights when I had to walk slowly between the grey build-ings, my body pressed up against the wet stone walls, their frescoes obscured by the fog. Nights on which no one rode their bikes, and the sound of heavy footsteps was the only sign of other people about, when it seemed no matter how long I walked, I would never reach my cold house.

·

No matter how much time passes, there are some things she will never be certain of.

That day, why did the white dog flattened against the hot tarmac bite her?

When that was his final moment.
Why had he torn at her flesh so forcefully, using all his strength?
Why had she tried, so foolishly, to embrace him until the end?

·

"Can you hear me?"

She is listening to him intently. He doesn't know how difficult that is. She is looking at him intently. He doesn't know how difficult that is either. She is looking, with all her strength, at his face, which is nearly half in shadow in the desk lamp's slanting light.

"Are you listening over there?"

———

She watches him get to his feet. She watches him approaching her, in his white shirt whose splattered bloodstains have now stiffened into dark brown patches, moving his feet with care. She sees that he is even more exhausted than she is, that he is struggling not to stagger.

.

"I'm sorry.
This is the first time I've spoken at such length by myself."

He just about manages to push the fatigue to the back of his face and speak. He bends forward and reaches out his left hand toward her. She looks into his eyes that are no longer behind glasses. These are eyes that distinguish dark and light, eyes that are clearly looking at the contours of her face.

"Will you write an answer here?"

She looks at his eyes that are no longer searching the empty air, but are the eyes of someone who has been speaking alone for a long time, the eyes of someone who has not heard a single answer.

"Would you like to call a taxi now?"

She moistens her lower lip with the tip of her tongue. She pulls her lips apart, then forcefully presses them back together. Supports his outstretched hand with her left hand. And with the irresolute index finger of her right hand, writes on his palm.

·

No.

Strokes and dots, faintly tremulous, brush over their skin simultaneously, then disappear. Soundless and invisible. No lips or eyes. The tremor and the warmth soon vanish. Not a trace remains.

I will take

the first bus.

20

Sunspots

He opens his eyes at the sound of heavy rain. It is dark. The window is open. He has to close it or the rain will keep blowing in. Absentmindedly groping on the desk next to the bed for his glasses, he recalls the events of the previous night. His right hand is still smarting.

He shifts himself off the bed and stands there in his bare feet. He heads toward the window, arms out, toward where the cold rain and wind are coming in. He strains to distinguish between the lighter and the darker darkness. He reaches to the side, to the front, but is still nowhere near the wall. Still nowhere near the radiator, or the bench beneath the window. Eventually, he feels the moist air on his face and arms. Droplets of water touch his outstretched hand. Gliding his way over to the window, he finds its aluminum handle. He slams the window shut. Water splashes his hand. The loud sound of rainfall retreats.

It doesn't take long for him to realize that the woman is not on the bench. There's no hint of movement or breathing. "Have the buses started running, then?" he mutters out loud. His voice sounds hoarse, like it belongs to someone else.

He sits on the bench. Passing both hands over its length, he discovers that the woman has left the thin quilt and blanket neatly folded. He had fetched them from the chest of drawers the night before. He lies down on the folded quilt. There is the faint smell of sweat, and an apple scent. It reminds him of bath soaps for young children. He raises his hands. The whitish thing is the bandage on his right hand; the less whitish thing is his left hand. The warm strokes and dots that had tickled over his left palm, the flesh remembers first.

The hand that hesitated, trembling ever so slightly. The fingers whose nails were clipped so short, they didn't hurt his skin at all. The gradually revealed syllables. The full stop like a thumb tack without the pin. The single phrase slowly becoming clear.

You probably wouldn't have guessed, but I've sometimes imagined sharing a long conversation with you.

I've imagined your listening attentively when I speak to you, and vice versa.

When we were waiting together in the empty classroom for the lesson to begin, there were times when I felt as though we really were conversing.

Then I'd raise my head and find you looking like someone half, no, around two thirds, no, more broken even than that—as wrecked as a mute object that has barely made it through, a ruin. At times I feared you. When I conquered that fear, went over to you and sat on a nearby chair, it seemed you would also move closer to me.

———————

There were nights when I thought of that frightening silence of yours. A silence entirely different from R's, as R's silence had felt like an immense pool of undulating light. Yours was like a hand under ice that had turned stiff after slamming in vain at the frozen surface. A silence like a snowdrift blanketing a blood-stained body. I was genuinely afraid that your silence would turn to actual death. Turn rigid, then glacial.

He opens his eyes and stares out into the darkness. He cannot see a thing. He closes his eyes again almost in submission, and looks at the darkness behind his eyelids. He gives his body over to the early-morning sleep that presses in on him through that darkness, impossible to defy. Hears the rain burrowing into his ears.

If snow is the silence that falls from the sky, perhaps rain is an endless sentence.

Words fall on to paving slabs, the roofs of concrete buildings, black puddles. Bounce off the ground.

Letters of my mother tongue, shrouded in black raindrops.

Strokes both rounded and straight; dots fading away.

Curled-up commas and stooped question marks.

In the dream he slips into as soon as he falls asleep, a dream that is at risk of disintegrating, he sees two people. An old man and a young woman. In a voice made tremulous by old age, the man asks, "Tell me, what is this smell?" Pressing his hands together in front of his chest, as though begging forgiveness.

The young woman begins to describe it. Swiftly, with animation, enthusiasm and accuracy. In alarmingly bold casual speech.

"It's a forest of oaks. The roots bulge here and there, sticking out of the ground like joints. There's an ivy wound tightly around them."

"What does it look like?"

"Trunks, crooked branches . . . like they might come for us, actually. Like they'd coil around us quickly and hurl us, but, oh—"

"But what? What do you see?" The old man's voice trembles. "Don't stay silent like that. Don't hide what's ugly and frightening from me. What's wrong? What's happening?" His words speed up. His voice grows more tremulous, higher pitched.

"Talk to me. With your lips, your tongue, your throat . . . speak. Where are you? Give me your hand, for God's sake, make a sound."

A sharp pain gouges his chest. He cannot catch hold of her hand. That woman, that woman's hand, is not here. He cries like a child. His eyes start open, and he discovers that he wept more copiously in the dream than in reality. There are only scant warm tears on his cheeks. Having found no solace, he is sucked down into sleep again.

This time it is not a dream but a memory.
The black bird that had come swooping down.
The stairs that had been sunk in darkness.
The glow from the flashlight that had pooled at the bottom.
The pale glimmer of her approaching face.

He starts awake from the memory.
And enters another dream.

———————

This time he is suddenly able to see clearly.

Strangers gathered in the cold depths of a subterranean space.

The warm breath billowing out of their mouths.

The white ash painted on each of their faces, as though they were corpses, or players in a farce.

A different dream steals in like a thief, blankets the first.

A rather dark stage.

People in their seats waiting for a performance.

The darkness that, instead of brightening, is growing gradually more deep.

The strange, long silence.

The performance that never begins.

Again the sound of the rain.

The darkened face of a woman from the past.

Cold raindrops.

On the umbrella,

on her brown forehead,

on her already wet hands. On the bluish veins swollen there.

A lucid, beautiful voice he is hearing for the first time speaks German words into his ears.

I told you, didn't I, that someday you yourself would become an impossible fallacy?

A familiar room wrapped in vibrant blue thread.

A letter dozens of pages long and composed of bright holes that he must now read.

Lying at his side and exuding cold,
     the indistinct contours of a person who smells of apples.

Trembling.

Palm.

A full stop.

Warm.

Black sand.

No, firm fruit.

In frozen earth

dug,

buried,

laid to rest.

A comma,

curved

eyelash,

frail

breath,

inside

a dark

sheath

inside

a shining

knife,

waiting

a long time

with bated breath,

He is jolted from sleep. Sits up. Realizes a sound outside his front door was what woke him up.

The unlocked door slowly opens. It gets a little brighter in that direction. Then darkens again, along with the sound of the door closing. Someone can be heard taking off their shoes. The rain is coming down heavily, but outside the window it is brighter than it was a little while ago, and with some guesswork he is able to make out the dark contours of a person. Seeing the dark form approaching, he raises his eyes. He scrubs his face vigorously with his unbandaged left hand, to remove the sleep. He inhales the distinct scent of soap coming from their hair as they draw nearer. He shivers, as though suddenly cold. Something white reaches out from the black form. Takes hold of his left hand and spreads it open. The other white thing slowly reaches out and writes on his palm.

It's time.
The optician's
will be open.

He reads the sentence through touch.

Do you have
a prescription slip?

He nods.

It's raining,
so I'll go.
It's best.

He waits some more. Waits for more words. Feels the cold moist air coming from her face, from her body.

———

The prescription—
    where is it?

He stands up, carefully disengaging his hand. He means to head to the desk, but abruptly, as though compelled, he moves toward the pale blur of her face, floating there in the dark. Raises his unbearably trembling left arm and brings his hand to her shoulder.

He doesn't know that her lips have stiffened as though her mouth has been gagged with transparent tape. He doesn't know that the previous night, she had been unable to sleep either in this room or after returning home on the first bus. He doesn't know that, after showering for a long time with warm water and her child's bubble soap, she had sat at the kitchen table and opened her Greek notebook. He doesn't know that she wrote out dead Greek letters as though feeling her way through dozens of forked roads buried beneath ice, and then, persevering, wrote beside them the unbearably alive phrases of her mother tongue.

With both eyes looking out into the darkness, he is still embracing her shoulders. He feels like he is weighing something and mustn't get it wrong. He feels he will surely get it wrong. It is truly frightening.

He doesn't know where she was directly before she came here. He doesn't know that she waited outside the school, on this last day before the start of summer vacation, searching the forest of umbrellas until eventually recognizing one with a picture of Buzz Lightyear, and her child's shorts visible beneath that, the brown spot imprinted on his knee, the size of a red bean. "Why are you here today? You know tomorrow's our day." That she stared down at the face of her child, who had whispered this as though he were afraid. That she wiped away the raindrops trickling down his face with the palm of her hand. That she had parted her lips in desperation, to call her child by his name, to say the words she had prepared. *You don't have to go far away. You don't have to go anywhere, you can stay here with me. We can run away together. We'll manage somehow.*

Her shirt is damp with rain and sweat. Leaving his bandaged right hand dangling in the air, he clasps her back a little more firmly with his left arm and hand, drawing her to him. Downstairs, someone bangs a door and stamps along the corridor.

He doesn't know that ropes of rain had crashed down on to her umbrella as she stood there in silence. He doesn't know that her bare feet had become drenched inside her trainers. "I told you, Mum, you can't just show up. I told you it's weirder to say goodbye outside." He doesn't know that the fin-soft flesh slipped away as swiftly as a fish when she moved to hug the boy, to catch his arm, to hold his hand. He doesn't know that spikes of rain sliced into the black puddles of rainwater like giant needles.

The sound of the rain edges in through the closed window. It is loud, strong—forceful enough to dent and fracture roads, buildings. Someone is dragging their feet as they walk down the stairs. Again, a door slams somewhere.

With their hearts pressed together, he knows her as little as ever. He doesn't know that a long time ago, when she was a child, she had looked out at the garden as the dusk was gathering, unsure if it was okay for her to exist in this world. He doesn't know the layer of words that was forever bruising her, pricking at her like needles. He doesn't know that his eyes are reflected in hers, that hers are in his reflection, and his again in those . . . in an endless reflection. He doesn't know how this terrifies her, and how her lips are clenched tightly for that reason, or that her lips are already blood-dark from the pressure.

In order to find the softest spot on her face, he closes his eyes and feels her face with his cheek. Her cool lips meet his cheek. A photograph he had seen long ago in Joachim's room, a photograph of the sun, flares up behind his closed eyelids. The surface an enormous burning flame, and over it dark patches that move. Sunspots, which explode and shift across the sun's surface, themselves reaching thousands of degrees Celsius. Were you to look at them from close up, through however thick a piece of film, your irises would burst.

He kisses her mouth without opening his eyes. Kisses the damp hair beneath her ears, her eyebrows. Like a faint answer heard from far away, the tips of her cold fingers graze his eyebrows, then vanish. They touch the chilly edges of his ear, the scar that runs from the corner of his eye to his mouth, then vanishes. Sunspots explode, without a sound, in the distance. Hearts and lips touch across a fault line, at once joined and eternally sundered.

21

Deep-sea Forest

We were lying side by side in the woods under the sea then.

In a place that had neither light nor sound.

You were not visible.

And I was not visible.

You did not make a sound.

And I did not make a sound.

Until you made a very small sound,

until a tiny, frail bubble emerged

from between your lips,

we lay there.

You were full of yearning.

It was frighteningly still.

It was dark,

as dark as the night that nightfall deepens to.

As dark as the deep sea where pressure flattens all living bodies.

At one moment, moving your index finger over the flesh of my shoulder, you wrote.

Woods, you wrote, *woods.*

I waited for the next word.

Realizing that no next word was coming, I opened my eyes and peered at the darkness.

I saw the pale blur of your body in the darkness.

We were very close then.

We were lying very close and embracing each other.

The sound of the rain did not cease.

Something broke inside us.

In that place where both light and voice were absent,

among slivers of coral that hadn't borne the pressure,

our bodies were now trying to float upward.

Not wanting to float upward,

I wound my arm around your neck.

I groped for your shoulder and kissed it.

So that I would be unable to kiss you again,

you embraced my face and made a small sound.

For the first time,

a sound as thin and frail as a bubble. And round.

I stopped breathing.

You went on breathing.

I could hear you breathing on and on.

Then we slowly floated upward.

First we touched the water's bright surface,

then we were roughly driven ashore.

It was frightening.

It was not frightening.

I wanted to burst out crying.

I didn't want to burst out crying.

Before you fell away completely from my body,

you kissed me, slowly.

My forehead.

My eyebrows.

My two eyelids.

It felt like I was being kissed by time.

Each time our lips met, the desolate darkness gathered.

Silence piled up like snow, snow the eternal eraser.

Mutely reaching our knees, our waists, our faces.

0

I bring my hands together in front of my chest.

I moisten my lower lip with the tip of my tongue.

Quietly, swiftly, my hands chafe.

My eyelids quiver like stridulating insect wings.

I open my lips, which are already dry.

I breathe deeper, resolute breaths, in, out.

As I speak the first syllable, I close and open my eyes with intention.

As if readying myself to discover, upon reopening them, that everything will have vanished.

Acknowledgments

I would like to thank Kim Suyeong for his Ancient Greek translations.

ABOUT THE AUTHOR

HAN KANG was born in 1970 in South Korea. A recipient of the Yi Sang Literary Award, the Today's Young Artist Award, and the Manhae Prize for Literature, she is the author of *The Vegetarian*, winner of the International Booker Prize, *Human Acts*, and *The White Book*.

ABOUT THE TRANSLATORS

DEBORAH SMITH was a co-winner of the International Booker Prize for her translation of *The Vegetarian*.

EMILY YAE WON is a translator based in Seoul. She has translated into Korean the work of Ali Smith and Deborah Levy.

ABOUT THE TYPE

This book was set in Garamond, a typeface originally designed by the Parisian type cutter Claude Garamond (c. 1500–61). This version of Garamond was modeled on a 1592 specimen sheet from the Egenolff-Berner foundry, which was produced from types assumed to have been brought to Frankfurt by the punch cutter Jacques Sabon (c. 1520–80).

Claude Garamond's distinguished romans and italics first appeared in *Opera Ciceronis* in 1543–44. The Garamond types are clear, open, and elegant.